The Cat's Got Her Tongue

Bobbie Montgomery

Pacific Press Publishing Association
Boise, Idaho
Montemorelos, Nuevo Leon, Mexico
Oshawa, Ontario, Canada

Designed by Tim Larson
Cover illustration by Sue Rother

Copyright © 1985 by
Pacific Press Publishing Association
Printed in United States of America
All Rights Reserved

Library of Congress Cataloging in Publication Data

Montgomery, Bobbie, 1918-
　The cat's got her tongue.

　Summary: When her family moves to the country, six-year-old Bea adjusts to her new home and overcomes her difficulty in talking to new people with the help of her belief in Jesus.
　[1. Seventh-Day Adventists—Fiction. 2. Family life—Fiction. 3. Behavior—Fiction. 4. Christian life—Fiction] I. Title.
PZ7.M764Cat　　1985　　[Fic]　　85-12155
ISBN 0-8163-0615-X

Dedicated to—

Molly Montgomery, my granddaughter, who from age two has criticized my stories interestwise.

Contents

1. Moving Day 7
2. The Snake 13
3. Rhodie's Chicks 17
4. Superstitious Grandma 23
5. Surprise Party 29
6. Puff Ball 35
7. Uncle Bill's Farm 39
8. Who Started the Fire? 45
9. First Day of School 49
10. Two Storms 55
11. What's a Twerp? 61
12. Stripe's Lunches 65
13. Runaway Puppy 71
14. A Lost Envelope 75
15. The Bible Meetings 81
16. Visiting an Enemy 85
17. "Let's Go, Daddy!" 91

1. Moving Day

Bea peeked out from the covers, remembering the family would move today. Months ago Daddy had teased, "Hey, town girl, how'd you like to be a farmer and have chicks, a cow, ducks, and the whole business?"

Bea thought it sounded great.

Daddy had pulled one of her curls. "Six years old is a good time to start farming. You and Dale can have a little garden and feed the chickens. You'll like the farm." All that had been months ago. Now, this morning, they were going to move to the farm, and Bea was scared. She looked around her room at the pink wall with baby lambs on it and her big window from which she could watch the street. Her chest felt tight, and she bugged her eyes out to keep the tears from coming. This would be someone else's room after today.

Of course she could take her Swiss clock, Siamese cat lamp, toys, and Mitzie, her little fox terrier dog; that was nice. But there was what Mama and Daddy called her problem. When she met strangers and even some people who were not strangers, she couldn't talk to them. It seemed as if her mouth locked up, and the more they tried to get her to talk the tighter it fastened together. Sometimes her whole body tightened up when she met new people.

That's why Bea felt so scared this morning. *Everyone*

would be strangers in their new home. She knew she wouldn't be able to talk to them.

She cuddled down farther in bed. It felt cozy and safe.

Smiths wouldn't live next door to them on the farm. Mr. Smith gave Bible studies to Mama and Daddy. Mama, little brother, and Bea went to Sabbath School with the Smiths. She liked Sabbath School. No one tried to make her talk there. They smiled and did the talking. Mama said she might join the Seventh-day Adventist Church, and Bea wanted to be a Christian too. Daddy believed Jesus would come soon, but he didn't say he might be an Adventist.

Mitzie barked at Bea's door, and Dale, her three-year-old brother, yelled, "Bea, Bea, Bea." He sounded like a B B gun.

"I'm coming," Bea called and jumped out of bed. She dressed quickly, ran out the door, grabbed Dale's hand, and with Mitzie yipping behind, dashed into the kitchen.

Mama laughed, "About time! Uncle Bill's here with the truck, and everything is about loaded for the move. Get washed and scoot to the table."

Daddy stuck his head in the door. "If we step on it, we can make the trip today. Then Bill and I can come back tonight, sleep here, and take the rest of our belongings in the morning."

"Good. I'll get halfway settled tomorrow," Mama replied.

After breakfast Bea ran next door to tell Mrs. Smith good-bye. She liked Mrs. Smith and never felt shy with her.

Mrs. Smith hugged Bea close and said, "Honey, Jesus wants to help children. He loves you. Remember to pray. Mama and Daddy aren't members of the church, and you're moving away from Christian friends. You be a good girl and help the family, remember Jesus, and pray."

Bea promised she would. Then she ran back to help Mama finish packing. As she went by the truck, Uncle

Bill leaned out the window. "Hello, Bea. How's my little niece? Has the cat still got your tongue?" Of course she couldn't answer. Those words always made her feel as if something was squeezing her body tight. She ran into the house.

At last they were ready to go. Daddy took Dale and Mitzie with him in Uncle Bill's truck. After Mama stuffed another bag in the back seat of the car, Bea sat in the front and squirmed her feet between two boxes of things on the floor. Then Mama started the car and followed the truck down the street. Bea waved at Mrs. Smith until they turned the corner.

Bea asked, "Is it a long, long way?"

"We'll be there by late afternoon." Mama smiled.

They soon left the city behind. It seemed to Bea that the scattered houses, trees, and fields flew by, and small herds of cattle and flocks of sheep followed them.

Bea colored in her color book and looked out the window again. She shifted her body. Her legs felt as if stickers were pushing in them. It must be a long way.

Mama had brought a picnic lunch, and at twelve o'clock they stopped to eat. Soon they started out again. Bea exclaimed, "Will we ever get there?"

Mama laughed. "We're over half way. It won't be long until you see our new home."

After much sighing, watching out the window, and wiggling, they followed Uncle Bill's truck up a gravel driveway to a square farmhouse with an upstairs. Bea cried, "We're here!"

She gazed at a big barn and a chicken house. Mitzie barked and chased some ducks in front of the truck. Dale pointed to a cow inside a fence which was attached to the barn. He said, "My cow, my cow." Everyone laughed.

The men unloaded the truck and car. Then they left to get the rest of their things.

"Come inside, children," Mama called. "Let's explore."

Bea found her room had kittens and flowers on the wallpaper. Dale's room had puppies and flowers. Bea thought, "The people who lived here must have had a little girl and boy."

Mama said, "We'll have another picnic outdoors." She pushed articles around in the food boxes, hunting for certain things. Soon they had a lunch ready and carried it outside.

"Three trees growing out of one trunk!" Bea exclaimed. "And a picnic table with a bench on each side!"

"And a swing!" Dale added.

They put the food on the table and sat down. Bea and Dale needed no urging to eat. "You're eating like two hungry bears," Mama said.

All at once Mama whispered, "Be very quiet and turn slowly toward the big maple tree close to the back of the house. We are not the only ones changing homes."

Bea looked from top to bottom of the tree. She couldn't see a thing. Then she followed with her eyes where Mama pointed to a pile of dried leaves in the fork of some branches.

Bea gasped as she saw an animal with a swirly tail disappear in the dried leaves. She watched the squirrel come out, whish along a limb, and dart into a hole in the tree trunk.

Mama whispered, "The hole is her den. She has babies, and she's moving them from the den to a summer home of leaves."

Soon the mother squirrel appeared with a tiny baby held firmly in her mouth. Quickly she leaped from the hole to a bough and to another limb to disappear in the leafy nest. She came from the nest without her baby, looked around, and leaped from one bough to another and soon came back with another baby. They watched the mother make three trips.

Suddenly Mitzie came bounding around the house. She sat in front of Bea doing her begging trick. Her little paws quivered as she sat up asking for a tidbit.

Bea moaned. "Oh, Mitzie, you frightened the mother squirrel."

Mama explained, "I don't think so. The squirrel's move is probably finished. I think she's giving her babies lunch now."

Dale laughed. "Squirrels have lunch."

"Why do they move?" Bea asked.

Mama said, "It's not healthful for babies in a dark hole, and squirrels are poor housekeepers. They must move or clean house. Maybe they're lazy."

Laughing at the squirrels, they went into the house with Mitzie following close at their heels.

Their beds were not set up, so Mama helped make a bed on the living-room floor for Dale and Bea. She put quilts and pillows on the couch for herself. She said, "We must straighten your blankets some. Your bed looks like a squirrel's nest. Now I'm going to lie down. I'm very, very tired."

While Mama rested, Bea and Dale ran upstairs and down. They inspected the kitchen and all the empty rooms. Bea discovered a little room under the stairs. Dale peeked in. "It's dark."

Bea said, "We can have this for a playhouse."

Dale repeated, "Playhouse, playhouse."

Mama called, "Come, you little squirrels, crawl into your nests and sleep. We'll be very busy when Daddy returns."

Daddy and Uncle Bill came the next day with the rest of the things. For days they arranged furniture, unpacked dishes, towels, clothes, and toys. Daddy got a job in the town nearby, so he could only help evenings.

Friday, Bea asked, "Will we go to Sabbath School tomorrow?"

Mama said, "We'll have Sabbath School at home. Maybe Daddy will be interested later. He didn't go to all the Bible studies; perhaps he doesn't understand. Right now he thinks it's very important to work every day he can, and that includes Saturday. He feels the family needs the money. Besides, it's expensive to move."

Bea remembered the Sabbath School teacher's saying,

"There's nothing in the world more important than loving and obeying Jesus."

She frowned. It sounded as if things were going to go wrong. This must be what Mrs. Smith talked about. Would Mama and Daddy forget Jesus?

2. The Snake

As the weeks went by, Bea knew Mrs. Smith was right. Moving changed things, but what could she do about it?

One day she sat in the swing moving around and around, keeping her feet on the ground. She stopped still and gazed up at the three cedar trees growing from one trunk. It seemed as if their long, peaked tops touched the blue sky as they waved in the breeze.

She wondered about the changes. She liked the farm. She loved the calf, the cow, and the geese. She liked to play in the old barn. But the Seventh-day Adventist church was twenty miles away, and Daddy had to drive their car to work on Saturday.

Our Little Friend came in the mail every week, and when they first moved, Mama studied the lesson with her and Dale every day. On Sabbath morning they dressed in their best clothes and Mama had Sabbath School. They sang, read Bible stories, and studied the lesson.

Bea sighed. One Sabbath Mama saw Lily Bell, their cow, running up the road. Of course, they couldn't let Lily Bell run away. They went outside and chased her back. Dale fell down, and Bea scuffed her new shoes.

Another Sabbath morning, in the exciting part of a Bible story, Mr. Thomas came to borrow a wrench. When Mama went after the wrench, he said, "I'm sorry to interrupt you. What's your story about?"

Bea couldn't answer. It was one of those times when she

got all locked up. She kept thinking, "I wish Mr. Thomas hadn't come. I must talk or I can't tell about Jesus."

Mr. Thomas said, "I guess the cat's got your tongue." Bea squirmed and closed her mouth tight. She couldn't answer.

That was the last time they had Sabbath School. As the weeks went by, Mama talked about Jesus often. She said, "Never, never forget Jesus loves you." But she didn't have Sabbath School anymore.

One day Bea wiped two big tears from her eyes and jumped out of the swing. She called Mitzie, "Come, Mitzie. Let's see if Dale's awake. Mama said we may pick blackcap berries."

Mitzie wagged her short tail as if she understood and followed Bea into the house. Bea took two small peanut-butter pails from the kitchen counter as Dale toddled up to her. He was all smiles after his nap.

Bea said, "Here's a pail. We're going behind the barn to pick wild blackcap berries."

Dale took the pail and gurgled, "Pail, little red pail."

Bea called, "Mama, we're going after the berries."

"All right, dear. I'll help later."

Bea took Dale's hand as they went out the back door and down the hard, beaten path. She said, "Maybe Mama will make blackcap cupcakes."

"Cap cakes, cap cakes," Dale repeated over and over.

Bea put her arm around Dale and hugged him. "There are our five fine geese in the field!" She laughed.

"Peck, peck, peck," Dale shouted.

The chickens were doing a low, throaty hum, and the turkeys ran to the fence; but Dale and Bea didn't stop. They followed the fence that made a half circle from the front corner of the barn to the back.

Their cow, Lily Bell, watched them while she switched her tail and chewed her cud. The calf nudged Lily Bell with her nose.

"She's a black Lily Bell," Dale said and ran around the fence.

THE SNAKE 15

Bea ran after him. She couldn't see, for the nettle plants behind the barn grew tall. She called, "Don't touch the nettles. They're mean. They sting like bee stings and make welts." She caught up with Dale and took his hand, leading him around more nettles to the berry bushes. She liked taking care of Dale.

They started picking from the bottom of a small bush. Bea said, "The bushes on each side of us are as tall as Daddy, and that's tall."

Dale repeated after her, "And that's tall."

Bea picked about a cup of berries. Dale had three berries in his pail and purple juice all over his face. He pointed at the ground and said, "Tail, tail."

Bea looked where he pointed. Her heart seemed to pound clear up into her throat, for a huge snake lay curled up in front of them. It looked many times larger than the little snakes she had seen in the garden. It had a big tan body with wavy dark-brown bands around it.

Maybe it would wake up! Maybe it would spring on them! Maybe it would bite!

Bea grabbed Dale's hand. "It's a snake!"

She looked around. They couldn't get away. Berry bushes grew on both sides of them, and the barn blocked their way behind.

Bea called in a frightened voice, "Mama! Mama!" Could Mama hear?

Mitzie might help, but she had run after rabbits before they picked any berries.

The snake moved.

Bea clutched Dale's shoulder.

Dale stared as if he couldn't take his eyes away from the snake. He exclaimed, "He's unwinding!"

Again the snake moved its long body in front of them. It began to make a coil. Dale pulled from Bea as if to go toward the snake. She held him firmly. Dale must not get bitten.

Bea prayed out loud, "Jesus! Jesus! Please help us! What shall we do?"

The snake raised the end of its tail. What were those ridges on the end of his tail? His tail made rattly sounds. When she heard the sounds the snake made, Bea stepped back as far as she could and pulled Dale with her.

Just then Mama appeared. She had a garden hoe in one hand and a small plant in the other. When she saw the snake, her smile disappeared and her face turned as white as the lilies in the yard. She dropped the plant and exclaimed, "Don't move!"

Mama raised the hoe up in the air and quickly brought its sharp edge down on the snake just behind its head.

Bea stared at the long snake without a head. "Mama, it has things on its tail."

As color came back into her face, Mama said, "Yes, it's a rattlesnake. It's poisonous. Thank God I came in time, and thank God the hoe was sharp."

Bea said, "Mama, Jesus sent you at the right time. I asked Him for help. We were afraid."

Mama hugged Bea and Dale close. "Yes. I planned to plant that geranium, but decided to see how you were doing first."

Quickly Mama helped the children fill the pails with blackcap berries from a bush far away from the snake. Then they went to the house.

Bea pondered, "Mama thanks God. She says Jesus loves us. Why doesn't she have Sabbath School anymore? Sometimes when I think of talking to Mama about it I get all locked up and can't say anything. I want to obey Jesus. What shall I do?"

3. Rhodie's Chicks

That evening Daddy removed the rattles from the snake's tail. He said, "You seldom find a snake like this around here. You may never see another one, but I don't want you kids wandering off where Mama or Daddy can't hear you call. You must keep your eyes open and pay attention to the trail in case one is around."

"We will," Bea promised.

The rest of the week, Bea and Dale often talked about how Jesus protected them from the snake. Bea thought they should obey Jesus. Jesus loved them.

Late one afternoon while Dale slept, Bea looked at the bottom of the sky. It seemed to touch fir trees in the distance. Yellow, orange, and red melted together as if the sky were on fire.

She jumped off the porch and ran to the rows of raspberry bushes where Mama was hoeing weeds. She called, "Mama! Mama! Jesus is coming! Look at the sky!"

Mama leaned on her hoe and looked at the sun. She said quietly, "No dear, it's only a beautiful sunset."

Bea said, "The Sabbath School teacher said, 'Jesus is coming soon.' She told us that before we moved here."

Mama answered, "Honey, we've lived here only a few weeks. Jesus is coming soon, but we don't know the exact time. We must be ready for Him anytime."

"We never have Sabbath School," Bea said.

"We'll start again," Mama promised.

One Friday afternoon, when it was almost time for Dale's nap to be over, Mama said, "Why don't you see if Dale's awake. Then you two may gather the eggs."

Suddenly Bea had an idea. She ran to get Dale. He woke up, and she helped him dress. Then she took a basket down from a nail in the back room to put the eggs in.

As they walked to the hen house Bea explained her plan. "Tomorrow is Sabbath. Let's keep Sabbath the way Jesus tells us to. We won't play. We'll look at pictures and talk to God, and maybe Mama will have Sabbath School with us. Maybe we'll go for a walk in the woods."

Dale said, "We like Sabbath, don't we?"

Bea squeezed Dale's hand. "Yes."

As they neared the chicken yard, Dale wrinkled his nose. "Bad smell."

Bea laughed. "A skunk sprayed somewhere. Mama said the smell would go away in a few days."

They went into the chicken yard. Bea got a can of grain from the feed room. The chickens gathered around them, making happy sounds as Dale sprinkled grain on the ground. "Peck, peck, peck, all gone," Dale announced.

"So now we'll gather the eggs," Bea said.

They went inside the chicken house and checked each nest. " 'Most every nest has eggs in it," Bea said, as they filled the basket.

Dale smiled. "Basket's full!"

Bea suggested, "Now let's feed Rhodie and her chicks." They got feed for Rhodie, set the eggs outside the fence, and shut the gate. Calling Rhodie, they went to her little house with a peaked roof.

"I wonder what's the matter with Rhodie. Her feathers are all sticking up," Bea said, watching the big red hen run around in circles, clucking in a frantic way.

Dale pointed to a yellow lump in the grass.

Bea ran to it. A baby chick lay flat on its back with its feet in the air. Close to it, another lay on its side. Bea looked around. She counted fourteen baby chicks, all lying down. Two more chicks foundered around in the grass and fell over.

"What's wrong?" Dale asked.

"I think they're dead," Bea said.

She called, "Mama, come see the baby chicks. They're all dead."

Soon Mama gazed at the little yellow balls of fluff lying in the grass. She gasped, "What could have happened? Sixteen dead. I wonder where the other two are."

Dale said, "Ol' snake ate 'em."

"I don't think so," Mama said. "No. There they are lying in Rhodie's house."

Bea looked away. She loved the baby chicks and felt like crying.

Mama said, "Come, get the eggs. Daddy will soon be here. Maybe he can solve the mystery."

While Mama prepared dinner, Bea and Dale ran out under the cedars. Bea pointed to the sun. "It's going down. When it is gone, we'll know it's Sabbath."

"Going now," Dale said.

"But not all gone," Bea murmured.

At the sound of a car they looked toward the driveway. "Daddy, Daddy!" Bea shouted. They ran to meet him. Bea took his black lunch pail, and Dale grabbed his hand.

"What have you sprouts been up to?" Daddy asked.

Bea explained, "Oh, Daddy, all of Rhodie's baby chicks are lying in the grass, dead. Mama said you might solve the mystery."

"You don't say!" Daddy frowned.

Daddy had things to talk over with Mama. He didn't go out to see the chicks, and after dinner he helped a neighbor load a truck with wood.

Mama said, "Tomorrow is another day. We'll show him the chicks in the morning."

Later, Bea asked, "Mama, may we look at your green book? It's Sabbath now."

Mama got a big book from the bookcase with the words *Bible Readings for the Home Circle* printed on the cover.

She handed it to Bea. Bea and Dale sat on the floor looking at the many black-and-white pictures in the book.

As they reached near the back of the book, Mama said they must go to bed. They turned the page to a picture of a little child petting a lion and a lamb. Dale patted the page, "Nice," he said. "Goodnight, lion and lamb."

In the morning the children got up in time to have breakfast with Daddy. Bea said, "Won't you look at Rhodie's chicks before you leave?"

"OK," Daddy agreed.

Mama went with them. As they approached Rhodie's little house, all stopped, and Bea gasped, "I guess they've been resurrected."

Dale laughed. "Rhodie's got a worm. They all want it."

"I can't believe it," Mama said. "They are definitely alive. Whatever is going on around here?"

Daddy laughed and pulled on Mama's long hair to tease her. "Hey, can't you smell something strange?"

Mama answered, "There's been a skunk around. You should have smelled it yesterday. It's not bad now."

Daddy laughed again. "Well, that smell put Rhodie's chicks to sleep, and when the smell cleared out, the chicks woke up."

"I'm glad, glad, glad!" Bea exclaimed, whirling around and around. "And it is kind of like the resurrection."

"Yes," Mama agreed.

After Daddy left and Mama finished in the kitchen, Bea asked bravely, "Mama, shall I get the books and lesson out for Sabbath School?"

"Not today," Mama replied.

"But, Mama, we want to thank Jesus for Rhodie's chicks."

Mama answered quickly, "Bea, Daddy believes in the Sabbath, but he feels we should do everything we can to save money. The farm cost a great deal. I don't have time this morning for Sabbath School. Daddy's coming home early, and we're going to Mrs. Day's orchard to pick prunes for canning."

Bea took a deep breath. She forgot about Jesus and felt naughty. She thought to herself, "I don't like Mrs. Day and I don't like prunes. I won't say one word to Mrs. Day all the time we're there, and I won't talk to anyone but Dale, even if I don't feel locked up inside."

4. Superstitious Grandma

In the afternoon, Daddy drove into the yard tooting the horn, and Mama came out with buckets for the prunes.

Daddy called, "Come on, you sprouts, climb in the back seat. Push those boxes over. They're for the prunes."

They were soon in Mrs. Day's orchard. Mrs. Day came out and talked to Mama and Daddy. Then she said, "Hello, Bea. Hello, Dale."

Dale said hello, but Bea couldn't. She had planned on keeping quiet, but plans or no plans, she couldn't say a word to Mrs. Day.

Mrs. Day said, "What's the matter, Bea? Can't you say Hi to a friend?"

Bea stared at her feet.

Mrs. Day said, "I know what's the matter. The cat's got your tongue."

Bea frowned. That thing about the cat again! She hated it.

Dale pulled on Bea's hand, "Come on, Bea." So Bea went with Dale exploring in the orchard until Mama and Daddy called them to go home.

As they rode along, Daddy said, "You'd better try to speak to people. They think you're rude when you don't answer them."

Bea didn't answer Daddy. She knew what he said was true, but she couldn't help it.

When they got home, Mama went to the mailbox. She

came back reading a letter. She smiled, waved a letter to the children, and called, "Grandma Adams is coming to stay a whole month."

Bea felt happy again. Grandma would go on long walks in the deep woods with them and tell exciting stories that happened when she was a girl with five brothers and many horses.

Sometimes Grandma told stories that frightened Bea, especially the one about black cats. She said, "You must never let a black cat run in front of you. If you do, something bad will happen."

If a needle or a straight pin fell on the floor, Grandma walked around it, making the sharp end point away from her. She would mutter, "I don't want needles and pins pointing at me, for surely trouble will come."

Grandma always stopped the rocking chair very still before she stood up. She said, "I must not leave the chair rocking while it is empty. That would bring sadness to the whole family."

Mama said, "Don't pay attention to Grandma's scary stories. She is superstitious. That means, everything frightens her. Needles! Black cats! Rocking chairs! How could they harm anyone? She should know better."

Grandma came, but the happy time didn't last. Little Dale got sick. He fretted all the time, either crying or waving his arms about. The doctor came often and gave Mama medicine for him.

Mama and Grandma acted serious. They whispered to each other and tiptoed around the house. Grandma never talked to Bea, except to say, "Run along and be a good girl."

When Daddy came home from work, he never yelled, "Where are my young sprouts?" He came in quietly and whispered, "Where's Mama?"

Bea spent most of her time going from window to window, looking out or swinging slowly under the three cedars.

Mitzie followed her everywhere. She seemed to know

SUPERSTITIOUS GRANDMA

Bea needed company. Bea petted Mitzie and talked to her. "It will be all right soon. Everyone will be happy again. Little Dale will be out playing with us."

One day someone left the screen door open. A little bird flew into the house. Grandma grabbed a towel and frantically waved it at the bird. She chased it from window to walls, into the kitchen and back out the door. She fastened the screen door securely and sank down heavily on the couch. She looked frightened.

Mama came out of little Dale's room. "What's the matter?" she asked.

Grandma said faintly, "A little bird flew into the house. Someone's going to die."

Mama looked unhappy with Grandma. She said, "Now, Grandma, we have enough trouble without that silly story. There isn't a bit of truth in it."

"You'll see," Grandma replied.

Days went by, and they took little Dale to the hospital. Mama and Daddy spent all their time with him. Grandma stayed home with Bea, but they never went for walks in the woods.

One morning Mama and Daddy came home. They looked sad. Daddy took Bea on his lap and said, "Bea, your little brother is gone."

"He's dead," Mama explained. "He won't be alive again until Jesus comes."

"He doesn't hurt anymore," Daddy consoled.

A minister spoke at the funeral. "Soon Jesus will be coming in the clouds and take His people to heaven. It will be the most wonderful sight you ever imagined. Dale will be alive again. He will come out of his grave, and we'll all meet Jesus in the clouds. You must keep God's commandments. You must be ready when Jesus comes."

At the cemetery they put beautiful flowers on Dale's little grave. The minister read from the Bible. Then they went home. Relatives and friends came. Everyone spoke kindly to Bea, but she felt more locked up than she had ever been in her whole life.

She went outside. Her cousin, Leon, followed her. He said, "Bea, show me your baby chicks and where the skunk came."

Bea couldn't answer.

Her cousin said, "The cat's got your tongue. My dad said a paddlin' would make you talk."

Bea turned away. She make up her mind she wouldn't ever talk to Leon again. She ran back to the house.

As the days went by, Bea thought about Grandma chasing the little bird out of the house. Grandma said someone would die. How could a bird cause Dale to die? Bea didn't believe that story. Jesus never let it happen that way.

Bea wanted to tell Grandma, but Grandma pursed her lips together tight and walked away if Bea mentioned Dale or the bird.

In a few days Grandma went home. The evening after she left, the minister and his wife came. They talked about the weather and the farm. They discussed Daddy's work.

Bea grew impatient. She wished they'd talk about little Dale. Mama always started crying if she asked about Dale, and Daddy acted gruff. She wished someone would ask about the bird that flew into the house when Dale was sick. Mama wouldn't. Daddy wouldn't. How would she ever know if the bird made little Dale die? She'd have to ask the minister herself. How could she? If she even looked at him she squeezed up tight.

Bea grew frightened. The lady was saying, "It's getting late." They would be leaving soon.

Bravely Bea stood up from her chair and walked over beside the kind-looking man. She gazed up at him but couldn't speak.

The minister put his arm around her. "What is it, dear?"

All at once Bea felt right. The minister was a nice man. He was God's man. She said, "When a little bird flew into the house, it made my Grandma afraid. She said someone would die. Mama said, 'That's a silly story.' Is that why my little brother died, or is that just a story?"

The minister smiled and gently lifted Bea onto his lap. "No, that is a false story. A small bird flying in the house could never cause your brother to die. Little Dale died because Satan brought sin into the world. Satan knows stories like that will trick us into believing lies. He does everything he can to keep us from loving Jesus. He wants to keep us from having a home in heaven."

He patted Bea on the shoulder. "The next time you see Dale, he will be happy. He will come out of his grave. You can take his hand and go to heaven with Jesus. There will be no one sick there. Never again will anyone die."

Without thinking about whether she could talk or not, Bea said, "Dale loved Jesus. Dale wanted to live in heaven."

The minister smiled. "You're going to be in first grade this year. Did I guess right?"

Bea smiled. "Yes, I'm going to learn how to read."

"You learn to be a good reader; then you can read stories about Jesus. You can read to Mama and Daddy. When Grandma visits, you can read Jesus stories to her; then she'll forget Satan's lies. You'll be a missionary."

After the minister left and Mama tucked Bea into bed, Bea thought, "I'll do what the minister said. I'll learn to read and be a missionary for Jesus." But before she went to sleep a scary feeling crept over her. She made fists of her hands and squeezed them tight. She whispered, "When I go to school the teacher will be a stranger. Must I talk to strangers if I learn to read? How can I? How can I be a missionary if I don't learn to read? What shall I do?"

5. Surprise Party

School wouldn't start for a while, so Bea decided not to worry about talking to all the strangers there. The problem seemed far away. Right now, she felt lonely without Dale. Sometimes the loneliness felt like a pain that would never go away.

She had her little dog, Mitzie, and took her for walks. They ran along paths together and explored, but it was sad without Dale. She talked to Mitzie, but she only wagged her tail and barked.

One morning Bea sat by the window wishing for a playmate. She wanted a party with games and children.

Mama interrupted her thoughts. "Bea, I'm not feeling well today. I'm going to let my work go for a while. I left my knitting bag down at Mrs. Day's. If you went after it, I could sit and knit. Could you ask for it?"

"I'll go," Bea said. "I'll speak right up and ask for your things."

She slipped her shoes over her bare feet and tied them quickly.

Mitzie whined and jumped around, ready to go. Bea said, "Come on, Mitzie. You may go too."

Mrs. Day lived down the hill and over a little bridge past the Thomases'. Bea remembered that when they picked prunes for canning, Mrs. Day had said that awful thing, "Has the cat got your tongue?" Bea knew she acted naughty that day. She decided she wouldn't be naughty today.

As she walked, Bea thought about Mildred Thomas. She had played with her two different times. She was older than Mildred, so it was easy to talk to her. Maybe Mildred would come out to the fence when she went by her house. The idea made her happy. She skipped along, watching the birds flit here and there. She saw calves in a field and stopped to smell some wild roses. When Mitzie ran too far away she called her back.

As she neared Thomases', just as she hoped, Mildred ran out to the fence with her two little brothers following. "Where are you going, Bea?" Mildred asked.

"I'm going down to Mrs. Day's to get Mama's knitting things. What are you doing?"

"I'm minding Timmy and Tommy while Mother puts the baby to sleep," Mildred replied.

Bea let the words pop out of her mouth without thinking. "I'm having a party at my house. Come and play."

After she said it, Bea quivered inside. Why had she said that, just because she wanted a party? Oh, well, Mildred had to help with the little boys. Her mother wouldn't let her come anyway. She'd go on pretending the party.

Mildred smiled happily at Bea. "I'll ask Mother. When is the party?"

Bea's heart thumped. What if Mildred came! She wouldn't! If she said the party was today, there wouldn't be time. She said, "The party will be at two o'clock. I must hurry."

Mildred called after her, "May Timmy and Tommy come too?"

"Yes," Bea answered. It wouldn't be polite to say No, even for a pretend party.

Bea continued walking. She paid no attention to Mrs. Day's little gray donkey as it walked along the fence.

When Mrs. Day invited her in, she shook her head and clamped her mouth together. She had to ask for the knitting bag. Why was she all locked up? Then she saw the bag on a chair and went into the room and picked it up.

Mrs. Day said, "Oh, you came after your mother's knitting. Bea, you must stop this no-talk business. Everybody has to communicate."

Keeping her glance down, Bea didn't answer but turned quickly to go home. Instead of calling Mitzie, she gave her a shove toward the road. Mitzie cocked her head to one side in surprise but walked along with Bea.

Bea looked straight ahead when she went by Mildred's house. "Of course Mildred can't come," she reasoned to herself. "Anyway, I should have locked my mouth when Mildred came out to the fence."

Bea acted quiet at home. Mamma asked, "Did something unpleasant happen to make you feel bad?"

She didn't answer Mama's question but said, "I talked to Mildred."

Mama smiled. "That was nice."

After lunch Mama settled into a comfortable chair to knit. "I don't feel very bouncy," she said. "That means, I'm going to play lazy this afternoon."

Bea went out under the three cedars to swing. Her toes seemed to touch the blue of the sky when she noticed people walking down at the road before the hill started up.

She scraped her feet on the ground, jumped out of the swing, and ran to the fence. She saw Mrs. Thomas carrying the baby, Mildred hanging on Timmy's hand, and Tommy running ahead.

Bea exclaimed to herself, "They're coming to a party. There isn't any party."

She didn't want to tell Mama about it, but she must. Oh, why had she invited Mildred to a party?

Bea looked again at the woman and baby moving like a snail toward the hill. She ran into the house. "Mama, Mrs. Thomas and the kids are coming up the road."

Mama said, "They must be coming here, unless they turn on the lake road. Maybe they're going on a picnic."

Bea hung her head and said softly, "Mildred said they might come."

Mama exclaimed, "She did! How strange! They never go visiting."

Bea knew she must speak quickly or she'd be afraid to tell Mama at all. She blurted out, "I invited them to a party."

"A party!" Mama gasped. "Where?"

"Here," Bea mumbled.

"When Mama doesn't feel well? Why, Bea! A party means cake or cookies, something special. Come on! We can't disappoint the children, even if you have been naughty."

Mama talked while she put things out on the counter in the kitchen. "I'm glad I made a cake yesterday, although it's plain, no frosting. I'll put this whipped cream on it. It's a good thing Daddy always wants lemonade when he comes home from work, so I have some made. I'll add a few drops of food coloring to it and the whipped cream. Pink lemonade and pink frosting look like a party."

How Mama hurried! She rushed into her bedroom and changed into a pretty flowered dress. She told Bea to put on a nicer dress, not her best one though.

They were ready just in time to answer the knock at the door. Mrs. Thomas breathed hard from carrying the baby up the hill, and the baby cried; but Mama soon had everyone comfortable.

Bea pretended to wake her dolls up, and Mama got Dale's toys out for the boys to play with.

After Mama and Mrs. Thomas talked awhile, they put the cake and lemonade on the table under the three cedars. Bea brought little chairs for the boys to sit on. The girls sat on a small log in front of the flowers, and Mrs. Thomas sat at the table with the baby. The cake and lemonade tasted good.

Mama never once mentioned that the party was a surprise to her. She helped the children play games and talked with Mrs. Thomas. Everybody had a good time.

Bea thought the ending might be happy, but when the company left, Mama had to lie down on the couch. She said, "Bea, bring me a cold cloth for my head. I don't feel a bit well."

Mama stayed in bed for two days. Bea did everything Mama asked her to. She gave Mama medicine and ran errands. She helped Daddy feed the animals. She tried to be very quiet in the house. She often wondered if Mama would punish her for the party, but she didn't.

The day Mama got up, Bea laughed with joy. She ran out under her cedars. She raced with Mitzie and called to the sky, "Mama is all right."

However, She couldn't help thinking about the party. She must talk to Mama about it. "Mama," she began, as she sat by her on the porch. "I'm sorry I invited Mildred to a party. It made you sick."

Mama put her arm around Bea. "I know you get lonesome with little Dale gone. We all do. After this, please plan things with Mama first. I didn't feel like a party. Also, we should have time to get ready for a party. You did wrong inviting them to a party without asking me; however, I believe you've been punished enough."

That night Bea prayed, "Dear Jesus, please forgive me for inviting Mildred to a party when there wasn't any. Jesus, help me keep my mouth locked at the right time and unlocked when I'm to be a missionary. Amen." Bea sighed on the Amen and continued her prayer. She said, "Jesus, Mitzie and I are so very lonesome. What shall we do, Jesus?"

6. Puff Ball

One evening, after Mama began feeling better, Daddy pulled Bea onto his lap. He said, "This farm has a cow. This farm has chickens. This farm has a dog. We need a cat. Every farm, small or big, needs a cat. How about it, young sprout? Would you like a little black-and-white kitten, mostly black with a white tip on its tail?"

Bea bounced up and down. "Oh Daddy! Could we?"

"Yes, we could. Joe, the man I work with, owns a mother cat with kittens. He gave all the kittens away but one. Tomorrow I'll tell him we want it. Then he'll bring it day after tomorrow."

The day for the kitten to come arrived. Bea could hardly wait until Daddy came home with it. She took Mitzie for a walk down to the little creek. She jumped from one rock to another along the edge of the water, trying to catch a big green frog. The frog jumped every time she came close to him. He finally jumped on a rock far out in the water and gave Bea a defiant croak.

"I don't want you anyway," Bea said. "I'm going to have a kitten." She called Mitzie, "Come on, Mitzie. Come, let's go."

She asked Mama, "What time is it?"

She went out under the three cedars to swing. She tried to touch the blue of the sky with her toes and pretended when she swung back that she sat on a white cloud, but she didn't want to swing anymore. She wished the time would pass quickly. She ran into the house and asked, "Mama, what time is it? When will Daddy come with the kitten?"

She played nurse with her dolls. She put them in a hospital for special care, but finally quarantined every one of them with a smallpox sign. Then she pretended to hire a special nurse to take care of them and left. She asked, "Mama, what time is it?"

Mama said, "Six o'clock will come faster if you work. You may help me today."

Bea helped get lunch. She helped with the dishes. She helped Mama pull weeds out of the garden. Then they folded dish towels.

They sat down to rest, and Mama read stories to Bea. After the last story in the book, Bea said, "We've done many things. Isn't it time for Daddy to come?"

Mama laughed. "It's time to get dinner. It won't be long now."

Bea put the dishes on the table for dinner. She put napkins around and shelled peas for Mama's salad. She listened. She heard the car. "Daddy's here!" she yelled and raced from the kitchen through the front room onto the porch, and instead of going down the six steps, she jumped from the side to the ground. One bare foot hit a small stone. Her right foot came down on an upturned pitchfork. The middle prong stuck into the bottom of her foot.

She fell crying, "Oh! Oh!"

Mama and Daddy rushed to her. Daddy pulled the pitchfork out of Bea's foot. He said, "I'm glad it didn't go in any deeper. Mac's boy borrowed this fork a few days ago. When he brought it back, he must have thrown it here. That was very careless."

Daddy carried Bea onto the couch. Mama washed her foot with smelly medicine and bandaged it. In a short time she felt better.

Daddy brought a big box and set it by the couch. Bea forgot all about her foot as she took the little black-and-white fluffy kitten out of the box. They became friends right away. The kitten cuddled close to Bea, singing happily in his kitten way.

Mitzie stood on her hind legs and sniffed the kitten. She stuck her tongue out and licked its face.

Bea put an arm around Mitzie and said, "We're three friends, Mitzie, my Puff Ball, and me."

For a few days Bea hopped on her good foot. One day she didn't need to hop anymore. She could walk on both feet. She went out to the three cedars with Mitzie and Puff Ball following. She sat down under the trees. Mitzie leaned against her, and Puff Ball jumped into her lap. Bea whispered, "Jesus did a great thing when He made animals for us to love and play with. They're easy to talk to. They keep me from being so lonesome."

Mama called, "Bea, come in."

Bea ran into the house with Puff Ball and Mitzie right behind her.

Mama said, "Daddy has the day off tomorrow."

Bea clapped her hands. "Oh, goody!"

Mama smiled. "We're going to Uncle Bill's big farm, so we must do extra work today, and you can help."

Bea exclaimed, "Oh, good! I'll help."

Bea wanted to go to Uncle Bill's. She liked playing with her cousins. She never felt all tight and unable to talk with them. She wished she could answer Uncle Bill when he talked to her. She hoped he would forget about the cat having her tongue.

7. Uncle Bill's Farm

The next morning Mama called, "Come, Bea, put your pets inside the backyard fence. They will be safe there. Give them plenty of food and water. We're going to Uncle Bill's now."

Bea took care of her pets. She said, "Now drink your water, and don't eat all your food at once."

Soon they started. Bea liked Uncle Bill's farm, but there were a few don'ts to go over before they arrived. Mama said, "Don't go where we can't hear you call. Raymond is seven years old and plays rough. He thinks it's funny to get you and the younger boys into trouble."

Daddy said, "Uncle Bill's farm is big. Don't go near the machinery. Don't get behind the horses, for they might kick. Don't climb things you can't get down from."

At last they arrived. Daddy helped Uncle Bill repair some of the machinery, and Mama visited with Aunt Lucy in the house. Bea played outside with her cousins. She never felt shy with them.

The boys showed Bea the new calves and the baby kittens. They petted the horses and took a sugar lump to the pony Uncle Bill had bought the day before. Bea helped gather eggs and feed corn kernels to the hissing geese.

Finally all four children sat down under a tree for a few minutes. Raymond, the oldest cousin, said, "I heard a wild duck down the creek this morning. Dad said she probably has little ducks."

Willie, the middle boy, exclaimed, "Come on! Let's find them."

They ran down the lane and climbed over the fence. They ran through the pasture and past the maple trees, around berry vines and brush, to the bubbly creek.

Raymond said, "Everybody be quiet, or we'll scare the mother duck and her little ducks."

They hid their shoes under a bush and waded down the creek on the shallow side.

Bea filled her pockets with wet stones until they leaked water. The bottom of her dress dragged in the water when they went through a deep place. She stumbled on rocks sometimes. Nothing bothered her, because she wanted to find the baby ducks.

They stopped, and Raymond piled large stones in a circle at the edge of the creek. The boys chased minows into the little pool the rocks made. Then they took the stones away, freeing the tiny fish.

Bea liked to watch the water skippers. She said, "The skippers look like spiders, but they skip instead of spin."

Harry, the youngest cousin, chased the skippers, but he couldn't catch any.

Bea noticed that the farther they went the larger the trees were. The big branches hid the sun, making it gloomy. She could hear nothing but the swishing water as they pulled their feet through it. "What happened to everything?" she asked.

Bea frowned and worrried. They were going too far. She should never have come to the creek. Why had she forgotten Mama's and Daddy's don'ts? She said to the boys, "We've come a long way. We'll never find the ducks. I'm all wet. Mama couldn't hear if I called."

Raymond laughed. "Then don't call her, and she won't need to hear you."

Bea replied, "Well, I might want to call her. Besides, she won't like it because I'm all wet. Will Aunt Lucy care if you're wet?"

"We'll dry before we get home," Willie said.

Bea thought about that. She knew Mama and Daddy wanted to know where she played. She said, "I'm going back."

"OK, scaredy-cat. You're mama's baby," Raymond teased. "You can't do anything. Your mama might not like it."

The boys laughed.

Bea ignored their laughter. She turned around and plowed back through the water. She was in a hurry now. She could hear the boys coming behind her, talking about babies who're always running to mama.

When they left the creek, they had nothing to dry their feet on, so they all carried their shoes. The bushes slapped Bea's wet legs. Her dress got dirty instead of dry. Her arms and legs itched. Her face smarted.

Raymond exclaimed, "I hear Mom calling us! She's mad! Let's hide in the barn!"

"Yea," Willie agreed. "She said she'd wallop us next time we got wet."

Bea ran with the others through the door of the barn. She followed the boys to a huge, high square box with a ladder nailed to the side of it. They climbed the ladder to the top and stepped into the wheat. It felt funny to Bea's feet, like being in sand.

"They'll never look here," Raymond gloated.

Willie said, "If they do, we'll catch it. Dad said to stay out of here."

Harry whimpered, "We'll get a spanking. I know we will."

Raymond growled, "Be quiet, bawl baby! Do you want them to hear us?"

Bea looked about. They were close to the ceiling. She could see huge beams and cobwebs. "It's fearsome," she muttered.

"Nobody can see in here," Raymond whispered.

Bea answered, "God can. He sees everything. He watched us all day. He knows right where we are."

Raymond piled wheat in a little pile and looked up at

the ceiling. "God can't see us. Look at those big beams. That's a thick roof. There are thick shingles on the outside. Nobody could see through that."

Bea explained, "God isn't just anybody. God made the world. God is great. He can see through anything. He even knows what you're thinking. He knows when you don't obey your parents. I'm going."

Bea put her shoes on and climbed out of the huge bin and down the ladder. Harry followed her, saying, "I like to be with you. You won't get into trouble."

Aunt Lucy was waiting for them near the bottom of the ladder. She had a long willow switch in her hand. She ignored Bea and Harry. She went right over to the ladder and met Raymond and Willie coming down. She switched the boys as they jumped from the ladder and ran to the door.

Mama came. She looked sadly at Bea and said, "I'm disappointed in you."

They went to the house. Uncle Bill and Daddy soon came in for dinner. Uncle Bill smiled at Bea, "Hi, Bea. You look sad. What's the matter?"

Bea didn't answer. She glanced away and started scratching her itching legs.

"Now, Bea, aren't you going to talk to your Uncle Bill? Can't we be friends?"

Bea couldn't say, "I've been naughty. I feel terrible. I'm not hungry, and I don't feel like being friendly. I'm locked up inside. I can't talk."

As they sat down at the table, Raymond said, "Remember, the cat's got Bea's tongue."

Willie remarked, "She talks to us."

Aunt Lucy said, "That's enough, boys. Be quiet."

Bea frowned and picked at her food. That was the first time the boys ever mentioned that cat business. She had supposed they were her friends.

After dinner Mama, Daddy, and Bea started home. Bea sat between Mama and Daddy in the front seat of the car. Mama said, "Bea, I warned you about Raymond. You went too far, and I could never hear you call from the creek. You will be punished too."

Bea hung her head. She knew she had been naughty.

Mama went on talking, "You will be punished in a different way. You are scratching your arms and legs. Your face is red. Do you know why?"

Bea shook her head.

"Poison oak is a plant with shiny green leaves that sometimes become red. They are pretty, but if you touch the plant, it poisons you. You get little bumps that are very very itchy. If you keep scratching, the bumps spread. Sometimes you get blisters and bad sores. You look as if you went through a lot of it. I'm sorry."

Daddy said, "Another thing, you're being rude to people. It's time you acted more grown up."

Bea felt miserable for days. Her body and face itched. The tiny red bumps all over her legs turned into blisters. She hated having the medicine put on. She decided Mama and Daddy's don'ts were important. She thought being a missionary meant more than learning to read. She must obey Mama and Daddy. Now Daddy was angry with her because she didn't answer when people spoke to her. How could she answer them? Especially when they said that awful thing about the cat!

8. Who Started the Fire?

Many days later, Bea looked in the mirror. She found no red splotches, bumps, or blisters. She yelled, "Mama! The poison oak's all gone. Look! Look!" She ran into the kitchen to show Mama.

Mama stood before the window gazing out. She said, "When Daddy comes this evening, we're going to a party."

Bea clapped her hands, "Oh, fun! And my face looks like me."

Mama looked sad.

"What's the matter, Mama? Don't you like parties? Don't you like my face?"

"Honey, of course I'm glad your face cleared up. About the party, it's different from any you have gone to. There will be music and dancing. From the Bible studies, I learned that such parties are wrong. Jesus wants us to stay away from things like that."

"Why are we going then?" Bea asked.

Mama looked away. "I can't disappoint Daddy. All his new friends will be there. He wants us to go."

Bea worried. "Won't God be mad if we go?"

"No, but He will be sad."

"I'm sad too." Bea sighed.

"There will be little girls to play with. You will have a nice time. Be a good girl."

Bea frowned. She knew Mama wanted to be like Jesus. Why did she do wrong things? Would Mama ever become an Adventist? Would Daddy always work on the Sabbath? They should have Sabbath School as they did at first. She didn't want to go to the party anyway. There would be strangers who knew that cat remark.

Daddy came home, and after dinner they got ready for the party. Bea thought Mama looked pretty in a new blue dress. In the light, her dark hair shone like many sparkling jewels.

At the party, Mama sent Bea to play with the other children in a room that opened into the big room where the dancing took place. There was a little girl there who smiled at Bea and moved over, giving Bea a place to sit. It was easy to make friends with her. She said, "My name is Doris. What is your name?"

Bea replied without being afraid, "My name is Bea." She found that Doris lived across the lake from her house and would be in the first grade when school started.

The other children were older. Bea was glad they paid no attention to her. She heard them talking about their school. They all seemed to be in the fourth and fifth grades.

Doris and Bea looked at the books on a table and watched the dancing from the door. The other children played games. Bea noticed the games always ended in a quarrel.

Billy pushed a checker board away from him and grumbled, "Who wants to play checkers? When do we eat?"

Another boy answered, "You know how it goes. They eat when the kids are too sleepy to be hungry."

Diane said, "Let's get something to eat now."

Bea counted ten children as they trooped into the kitchen. Doris took her hand, and they followed.

Jimmy, the largest boy there, looked at the big table in the kitchen loaded with food that each family had helped bring. He said, "Grab a paper plate and get what you want. Let's go outside and eat."

Bea looked around the kitchen. There weren't any grown-ups there. "Is it all right to eat?" she asked Doris.

WHO STARTED THE FIRE? 47

Jimmy heard and laughed. "Sure, that's what the food is here for."

The children piled their plates high with little sandwiches, olives, cookies, and cake. Then they went out the back door, down a little hill, and sat in the grass under a large tree. Everyone enjoyed the food and being outside.

Bea liked sitting under the tree, even if the dry grass scratched her legs. She hoped poison oak didn't grow near. She couldn't be sure in the moonlight.

Jimmy said, "I've got matches. Let's burn our plates; then no one will know we ate early. We'll eat again when the rest do."

Soon the boys had the plates burning in a fire. A slight breeze made the flames dance. They swooped back and forth and finally went out in a pile of ashes.

Bea sighed in relief. "I'm glad the fire went out. Doris, let's go back. My Mama and Daddy will wonder where I am." The other children followed.

One of the boys yelled, "Hey, look! The fire's started up again! It's burning the grass!"

Bea turned around. The flames wove back and forth, then up and down. She could hear them crackling in the grass. She exclaimed, "We must call our parents quick! Come on, Doris."

Diane yelled, "They're going to tell. We'll all get into trouble."

The grown-ups were busy talking, laughing, and dancing. The girls had a difficult time getting their attention, but Mama listened and explained to the others.

"Burned the paper plates!" boomed Jimmy's father. "I'll strap that kid."

The parents hurried out past the girls. When Doris and Bea caught up, the men had tramped the fire out, and Jimmy explained, "Those little twerps started the fire and ran to the house."

Jimmy's big father yelled, "What twerps?"

"Them." Jimmy pointed at Bea and Doris.

The man asked the rest of the children, "Is that so?"

Everybody was looking at Bea and Doris. "Yeah," several of the other children said.

Bea clutched Daddy's hand. Why did they say that? They knew who started the fire.

Daddy looked right into Bea's face.

Bea felt all squeezed up tight. She couldn't speak to Daddy. She couldn't tell him the truth. She just shook her head.

Daddy smiled reassuringly at her. She knew he believed her when she shook her head.

The children glared at Bea. She wondered why. They knew she didn't start the fire. They knew Doris didn't either.

Jimmy's father said loud and clear, "That's an unlikely story. These two little girls didn't have matches. I doubt if they could start a fire. You big kids get into the house and behave yourselves, or you're going to hear more about this."

The next afternoon, Daddy said, "Bea, you knew Daddy wouldn't want you to go out in the dark without a grown-up. You didn't start the fire, but you were with the big kids that did."

Bea agreed. "I know, Daddy. We should never have gone to a party like that. Jesus didn't want us there."

Daddy smiled. "Maybe that's true, but you should obey me."

Bea said, "I know I should, because I'm going to be a missionary for Jesus."

Daddy patted her shoulder. "You're going to be in first grade soon. You'd better start acting like a big girl. Did you talk to any of those kids?"

Bea muttered, "Just Doris. We're friends now."

"I'm glad you have a friend. You'll be in school together."

Bea got that sinky feeling about school again. There would be a building full of strangers. Did school start soon? What could she do? Did she have to go? Couldn't she learn to read at home?

9. First Day of School

Bea talked to Daddy about the idea of learning to read at home. "Mama could teach me," she said.

Daddy laughed. "You're going to school, sprout. Everybody goes to school. Besides, you'll like it. Believe me! You'll get over that problem of yours too."

A few days later, Mama and Bea rode with Daddy to town when he went to work. They planned on shopping for school. Bea could hardly believe it. She would be in first grade. She would learn to read. Daddy said she would learn to be friendly with people. She became so carried away with plans that she forgot about meeting strangers at school or being all tight if she must talk to them.

First, they bought a warm coat for Bea with five gold-colored buttons down the front. Then she tried on many pairs of shoes and finally decided on brown ones with shiny gold hooks that matched the buttons on her coat.

They went to a store with bolts and bolts of material for dresses. Mama talked to her about which materials would wrinkle and which would get dirty easily. They talked about what color looked nice with brown eyes and brown hair, and which would be best for school.

They chose a red piece of material, a bright blue one, a red plaid one, a piece with many colored flowers, and one with bright green stripes.

Bea wished the clerks would stop trying to make her

talk to them. They might spoil everything, for she couldn't answer.

Mama and Bea had lunch in a restaurant. Bea saw other children with their mothers. Mama said they had been shopping for school too.

Later they looked for a lunch box. Bea wanted a black one like Daddy's, but Mama said the pretty square ones were for little girls. She got a shiny blue one with a picture of a gray kitten on it. Pink flowers peeked around the kitten and seemed to tickle its nose.

Next Bea chose school supplies. She got a box of crayons with three rows of bright colors, four pencils, and a tablet with wide spaces between the lines. The cover had a dog picture on it that looked like Mitzie. She got scissors and paste, but best of all a bright red pencil box with erasers and a ruler in it.

Mama said, "When we get home, we'll put your name on all of your things."

The shopping finished, they waited for Daddy in a little park. "Whee!" It was fun going down the slide.

Bea threw flat pebbles in the little creek that ran by, gurgling on its way. The pebbles made splashy sounds, and sometimes they made plunk sounds.

Mama never mentioned that she must keep clean, so she took her shoes off and rolled in the tickly grass. How nice it felt after all the walking and standing in stores.

When Daddy came, Bea talked all the way home about her packages.

Daddy laughed. "After buying all those things you must work hard at school, obey your teacher, and answer when she speaks to you."

Bea frowned. A teacher wouldn't say that horrible thing about the cat. Perhaps the teacher wouldn't even speak to her. School would turn out all right.

Feeling happy again, she smiled at Daddy. "I'm going to try. I'm going to learn how to read. I'm going to be a good reader. I want to read Jesus stories to you and Mama. We will all love Jesus more and do what He tells us. Next time Grandma Adams comes, I'll read about Jesus to her; then she won't be afraid of everything. Remember the minister that came to our house? He said I could be a missionary when I learned to read."

Daddy raised his eyebrows. "You certainly have big plans."

The first day of school arrived. Bea looked at the row of new dresses Mama had made for her. She decided to wear the red one with bunny pockets.

What an exciting day! She carried her shiny blue lunch box and red pencil box carefully. Mama brought the crayons and paper. Bea liked her teacher. She had red hair and a kind smile. She showed Bea where to sit. Mama helped arrange her things. Everything seemed nice until the bell rang and all the Mamas disappeared; then Bea felt lonely. She must not cry.

The teacher said something to each child and asked their name. Then she looked at Bea and wanted to know her name.

Bea thought, "She knows my name. I heard Mama tell her." Bea stared at the top of her desk. Daddy told her she had to answer the teacher's questions. She couldn't. The teacher smiled and started talking to someone else. Oh, she should have said her name. Everyone else told their names. She wanted to run out the door and find Mama, but she couldn't, for she must learn to read. She wanted to be a missionary.

She felt better when she glanced across the room at a little girl. The girl smiled. Bea smiled back. It was Doris, the girl she had played with at the party.

They sang songs, and the teacher read them a story. Then they went outside to play. Doris and Bea took hold of hands and skipped around together. Bea liked having a friend.

After recess they colored a picture. Then they counted little sticks and played a game.

They ate lunch in another room. It had long tables and benches in it. Bea sat by Doris. She opened her new blue lunch box and took out all the little packages. Mama had thought of everything. She had even started peeling the orange for her.

After lunch Bea and Doris went outside again. They played on a slide and swung in the swings until the bell rang. Then back to their room they went.

Bea disliked lying on her little rug to rest, but she enjoyed the story the teacher read.

At the next recess, outside, Doris talked to the teacher a few minutes. Bea liked the teacher and wanted to be friendly, but she couldn't. She felt afraid. She wandered to the edge of the playground, under some large trees. She picked up a black-and-orange caterpillar. She let it crawl on her hand; then she put it in her bunny pocket. She saw another one and put it in her pocket. She collected more black-and-orange caterpillars until one pocket bulged. Then she started putting caterpillars in the other pocket. When the bell rang both pockets felt heavy.

Everyone settled down, and the teacher passed out little books with dot-to-dot pictures in them. Bea knew how to do that.

Soon Bea felt a lot of squirming going on in her little bunny pocket. One of the caterpillars came crawling out on her lap. Another came, feeling its way down her leg.

Oh, dear, she shouldn't have brought them into the classroom! When she tried to put one back into her pockets, more came out. She couldn't move, for they might get smashed. Soon many black-and-orange caterpillars crawled all over her lap and down her legs and up the front of her dress.

The little girl who sat across the aisle from Bea ran to the teacher and whispered in her ear. The teacher came to Bea's desk. "Oh, my!" she exclaimed and hurried to the cupboard, returning with a box.

By that time the children were out of their seats, standing around watching the caterpillars, squealing and yelling each time another one crawled out of Bea's pockets.

FIRST DAY OF SCHOOL 53

Bea asked herself, "Am I going to get into trouble my very first day of school?" She tried to keep the tears from coming to her eyes.

The teacher said quietly, "Let's put them all in this box. Be careful where you walk. You might step on one."

The children helped put the furry little orange-and-black caterpillars into the box. They seemed to like it there, for they quit crawling and trying to get away.

The teacher smiled. "If you children will sit down nice and quiet, Bea will bring the box around, and you may all see the caterpillars again before she takes them back to wherever they live."

After Bea took them outside, the teacher read from a book how caterpillars spin a home around themselves and in the spring come out of their home as butterflies and fly away.

The teacher asked, "Bea, where did you find the caterpillars?"

Bea squeezed her hands together tight. The teacher was nice. She didn't get angry about the caterpillars, but Bea couldn't answer her. She looked down at her hands and then up. Everyone stared at her.

The teacher said, "Were they under the trees?"

Bea nodded her head.

That evening Bea told Mama and Daddy about school. "I didn't learn to read though," she complained.

"You will," Mama comforted her. "By the time the caterpillars are beautiful butterflies you will be reading."

Daddy questioned, "Bea, did you answer the teacher when she spoke to you?"

Bea's face flushed red. She felt ashamed. "Daddy, I will tomorrow. Honest, I will."

10. Two Storms

Bea failed to answer the teacher when she spoke to her the next day or the next or the next. Every evening Daddy asked, "Bea, did you answer Miss Harvey when she spoke to you today?"

Every evening Bea replied, "I will tomorrow, Daddy. Honest, I will."

Daddy's voice got more firm each day, and Bea felt more ashamed each day; but she couldn't speak to the teacher or to anyone else except Doris. For three weeks she dreaded having anyone speak to her.

One day some of the children complained about it being too hot. Miss Harvey said, "I have all the windows open except this one by my desk. It seems to be stuck, but I'll try again to open it."

Bea watched the teacher push and pry and finally get the window up a way. Then something happened. The window came down, and Miss Harvey made a pitiful little sound of pain, for her arm was caught under the window.

The children rushed up to the window and stood around talking and saying, "Oh," and other useless things.

Without stopping to think, Bea ran to the door and called to the janitor who was walking down the hall, "Mr. Johns, Mr. Johns, help the teacher! Her arm is caught in the window. Hurry! She hurts terribly."

Mr. Johns came into the room and crowded through the children to the window.

Bea spoke loud, "Mr. Johns will help the teacher."

Mr. Johns pushed the window open, and the teacher pulled her arm away.

Bea crowded up close to the teacher. She said, "My mama puts cold water on me to make things quit hurting."

Miss Harvey said, "Thank you, Bea," and hurried out of the room.

Mr. Johns suggested they surprise the teacher by being busy when she returned.

In a little while Miss Harvey came back. She said, "What good workers I have. Bea, thank you for the suggestion. The cold water helped." Then she asked, "Who called Mr. Johns in?"

Several children answered, "Bea did."

The teacher looked at Bea in surprise. She said, "Isn't that wonderful? Bea knows what to do in an emergency." She smiled at Bea. "Would you like to be a nurse when you grow up?" Bea smiled back and said, "Maybe, but I really want to be a missionary and tell people about Jesus."

Miss Harvey said, "You could do both."

Bea felt no tight bands squeezing her. She loved her teacher. She could talk to her. She said, "Maybe I'll be both, but I can start being a missionary when I learn to read."

After lunch, as it neared three o'clock, Bea thought, "It's the hottest day ever." She blew hot air from her mouth upward, making her bangs fly about. She scooted from one side of her chair to the other side. She looked at the teacher and the boys and girls. At last the bell finally rang.

By the time Bea reached home a strange thing happened. The sun disappeared. A big wind made the leaves hurry and the dust swirl around. Mama told her to gather up things like the rake and the wheelbarrow and put them away, as she expected a storm.

Daddy came home early. He put the animals in the

barn and fed them. He milked Lily Bell and hurried to finish his other chores.

Bea switched on the little kitchen radio. Only loud crackles and bangs came out of it. She turned it off.

After dinner Bea could hear the wind flapping the branches of the three cedar trees. Would they break off? Would they break the windows?

A crash shook the house. "There goes one of the big maples," Daddy exclaimed. "This wind may blow the cedars and the fir onto the house next. It's dangerous here. We'll take some blankets and stay in Jack's old log cabin tonight. It's built strong, and the trees that grew near it have been cut down."

Mama didn't say a word. She handed Bea her coat and started piling blankets in a heap.

Loaded with blankets, Mama and Daddy and Bea started out into the storm. Mitzie stayed close to Bea, touching her as they walked. Puff Ball dashed in front of them, going toward the barn. Bea's voice died in the wind as she called, "Puff Ball, Kitty, come with us."

"Puff Ball can take care of himself," Daddy said.

Mama warned, "Hurry. We mustn't be caught out here. It's going to get worse."

Daddy could hardly open the door of the cabin. It hadn't been used for a long time. With the help of Mama and Bea, he managed to open it wide enough for them to get in.

Mitzie followed Bea around the crude cabin while Mama and Daddy made a bed on the floor.

The wind, the dark, the rain, the fierce thrashing of anything loose all frightened Bea. She felt much safer cuddled between Mama and Daddy under the covers.

"Will the wind blow the cabin over?" she asked.

Daddy answered, "This is a strong, well-built cabin. I think it will stay up."

Bea heard the wind yowl and screech louder than ever. A loud crash split the air, and the cabin shook. "There goes another tree," Daddy said. "It sounded like a big one."

Mitzie crawled up close to Bea. Bea could feel her shaking through the covers. "Poor little Mitzie, you're afraid too," Bea sympathized.

Bea prayed silently, "Dear Jesus, be with us. Keep the cabin from blowing down. Take care of Puff Ball. Please don't let the trees fall on our house. We need our house. Take care of my three special cedars and keep them tall. Thank You, Jesus. Amen."

After praying, Bea closed her eyes and, in spite of the storm, went to sleep. It seemed only a short time when Daddy shook her shoulder. "It's morning. The storm's over, honey. Wake up! Mitzie's got a surprise for you."

Bea crawled out of the covers. "A surprise! Mitzie has a surprise! Mama! Daddy! Did Mitzie have her puppies?"

"Right over there." Daddy pointed to one of their blankets with Mitzie curled up nice as you please looking up at everyone as if the say, "This is something special."

Bea went over closer. "How many puppies, Mitzie?"

"Not puppies, but puppy." Mama laughed.

Bea looked down at the little white squirmy puppy with pink showing through fine hair on his legs, and black around one eye like Mitzie. "Mama! Daddy! Let's call him Storm. He came in a storm."

"Sounds like a good name," Mama agreed.

"OK by me," Daddy said. "He'll probably stir up a storm. Now let's get home and see what's happened around there."

They arrived home with little Storm wrapped up inside Bea's coat and Mitzie close as usual. Puff Ball bounded out from behind the house to greet them.

Bea looked at their home. It was safe and fresh after the storm. Her cedars were standing straight, tall, and clean. "Thank you, Jesus," she whispered.

Mama said, "Come on, Bea. You must get ready for school. You're a big girl now. School is your job."

Bea answered, "I will, Mama, and I'm going to tell about Storm at sharing time."

Daddy smiled encouragingly. "That's my girl."

On the way to the crossroads, Daddy said, "By the way Bea, do you remember the boy who started the fire at the party? Does he go to your school?"

Bea frowned. "I don't know. I hope not. I don't want to see him again." She felt frightened. Maybe he did go to her school.

11. What's a Twerp?

Bea raised her hand at sharing time. She said, "My dog, Mitzie, had a puppy, and I named it Storm." At recess time she told Doris all about spending the night in the cabin.
Ever since the day when Bea had called Mr. Johns to help the teacher get her arm out of the window, it seemed easy for her to answer Miss Harvey and enter into the fun with the other children in her room. She smiled at Mr. Johns when he spoke to her and never looked at her feet as if she were afraid of him. She still glanced down and got all locked up when other teachers besides her own spoke to her or when older children asked her questions.
But now she had another worry. Ever since Daddy asked her about the boy who started the fire at the party, she watched for him. When she saw a tall boy in a group, she got a sinky feeling in her chest. Could that be Jimmy? He might lie about her again or do 'most anything.
She asked Doris, "Does Jimmy go to our school?"
"Yes, he's in fourth grade. I'm glad they have recess and lunch at a different time than we do."
One Friday the teacher said, "The sixth-grade band from Town School will be here today. They will perform for us."
The entire school went to the program in the gym. Everyone sat on the floor facing the band. Bea could hardly keep her feet still. She wanted to march to the music.

Someone behind bumped her with his feet. She moved forward a little and continued to enjoy the program.

Later the music stopped, and the band leader stepped out in front to tell them he would come out to visit their school soon. Anyone from grade four up could take lessons on an instrument.

Bea put her hand on the floor and leaned to one side. She would learn to play one of those instruments someday.

"Ouch!" she cried and jerked her hand up from the floor. Somebody behind had jammed his foot down hard on her hand.

She turned around. There was Jimmy!

He grinned. "Hi, twerp."

Bea stared at him. He was a mean boy.

Jimmy laughed. "Can't you talk?"

Bea whirled around, keeping her hands safely off the floor.

That evening Bea asked, "Daddy, what's a twerp?"

Daddy said, "A twerp is a little person. Older kids and big people often call somebody younger a twerp. It's slang. Why?"

"A boy at school called me a twerp."

Daddy pulled Bea's hair a little and said, "He's probably just teasing. Don't pay attention to him. He won't have much fun then."

"Well, I don't like it. He's my enemy. He's the boy who said Doris and I started the fire at the party."

Daddy frowned, and Bea ran outside with Mitzie.

Many weeks went by. She didn't see Jimmy again until all the classes met in the gym for a sing. After the sing, her class passed Jimmy's in the hall. Jimmy looked at her, bugged his eyes, and said, "Hi, twerp."

Bea looked the other way, and Jimmy laughed. "Little twerp can't talk. The cat's got her tongue."

Bea bit her lower lip to keep from crying. She hated to have that said to her about the cat. Of course Jimmy would say it. What a horrid boy!

Later Bea complained to Doris, "Jimmy's a mean boy."

Doris replied, "Yes, but no one believed him at the party. His father didn't think we started the fire. My mother said so."

"I know," Bea agreed.

Bea walked with Doris to the crossroads on their way home from school. Doris turned to the left, and Bea went straight, as they lived across the lake from each other.

One afternoon the girls called good-bye to each other and Bea hurried along. She noticed that Tim Bryce, who went her way, had another boy with him. It was probably a friend going home with Tim to play. Soon the boys were right behind her. She glanced back and faced Jimmy. "Oh, dear," she thought.

"Hi, twerp," Jimmy teased. "Can you talk today?"

Of course Bea didn't answer.

Jimmy laughed. "Hey, did you see my dog? He's a big black one, and he's mean. He snarls and bites. If he comes near girls, they run and he chases them. Sometimes he tears their clothes."

Bea was frightened at first. She stopped in the road and looked both ways. She thought a second. She hadn't seen a dog. The boys snickered. She knew they were making fun of her. Jimmy didn't have a black dog.

Bea felt angry. She wanted to get even with Jimmy. She could trick too. She didn't feel locked up. She felt as if boiling water was bubbling over. She said, "I saw a big mean black dog. He came running after us. He bit Doris and tore her dress, and he chased her way up the road. I'll tell her mother who the dog belongs to. She'll be real mad."

Jimmy quit laughing. "Aw, you're a twerp, You never saw a dog. Besides, I don't have a black dog."

"You do. You said you did. You'll be in trouble too."

The boys turned on a side road and ran up a little hill out of sight.

"He's my enemy," Bea muttered to herself. She thought about it with each step. "I did wrong. Daddy told me to pay no attention to Jimmy. I shouldn't have said that about the dog. I made up a story. I should have stayed locked up as I always do. Why? Oh dear! Next time I see Jimmy, I won't act mad or pay attention when he calls me a twerp."

When she reached home, Mitzie ran out to meet her, and Puff Ball leaped right in front of her as she went into the house. Mama greeted her with a kiss. Bea picked up Storm and cuddled the wiggling puppy close. Home was safe and wonderful.

A few weeks later the weather was cold in the mornings, so Bea rode with Daddy to the crossroads, where he turned to go to work. Doris's grandpa now took her to school. It was agreed that Bea could ride with them from the crossroads to school. The girls could walk home, as it was warm in the afternoon.

Bea felt frightened at the thought of meeting Doris's grandfather. Would he say that thing about the cat if she couldn't talk to him?

12. Stripe's Lunches

The first morning when Bea climbed into the car beside Doris, Doris said, "Grandpa, Bea won't talk to you, but she's still friendly. She's my best friend."

Grandpa laughed. "Well, when Bea wants to be friendly with me, I'll be ready."

Something about Grandpa made Bea laugh too. Before she knew it, the tight bands around her were all broken, and she was having a good time talking with Doris and Grandpa.

One morning Grandpa seemed late. Bea jumped from one foot to the other trying to get her feet warm. Then she moved all around, jerking her body this way and that, as the teacher had shown them, to shake the wiggles out.

Suddenly she stopped. What was that? "Mew, mew, mew." Again, "Mew, mew." Bea watched as a hungry looking striped cat limped out of the bushes toward her. She squatted down and petted the cat and pulled burs from her fur.

"Poor kitty, one front leg's gone and someone cut half your tail off."

Seeming to like Bea's sympathy, the cat rubbed against her legs mewing again.

Bea opened her lunch box and broke one of her sandwiches in half. The cat didn't bother to sniff, but gobbled it down quickly. The peanut butter stuck to her throat, and she choked little chokes trying to get it down.

"I won't give you peanut butter this time kitty," Bea said. She broke off half of her other sandwich. The cat finished eating it as Grandpa's old Ford came around the corner.

Bea told Doris and Grandpa about the cat.

Grandpa said, "Poor kitty. She probably got caught in a mowing machine. When you saw her, was she healed up or still sore?"

Bea replied, "She didn't have any sores."

After school, Bea and Doris looked and called for the cat, but she didn't come. Bea hurried home wondering, "Will I ever see the poor kitty again?"

That evening when Mama washed her lunch box, she called to Daddy, "Would you look at this? The 'never-hungry girl' ate all of her lunch, every crumb!"

Daddy came behind Bea, put his hands under her arms, and swung her around. "You keep that up, my young sprout, and you'll start shooting."

Bea giggled. She liked having Mama and Daddy pleased with her. There had been times when they complained about the leftovers in her lunch box. She disliked telling them that she shared her lunch with the cat, but she must.

At that very minute someone honked a horn in the driveway.

Daddy said, "Oh, I forgot. I'm going to help Mac get his old truck started. It's about five miles out in the country. His wife is coming in to visit until we get back."

Daddy went with Mac. Mac's wife came inside and talked with Mama. Bea couldn't say anything about the hungry cat then.

The next morning, Bea jumped from the car and waved good-bye to Daddy. Soon the striped cat limped from the bushes and brushed up against her.

Bea petted the cat and opened her lunch box. She gave half of her favorite sandwich to the hungry animal. She took out a pretty small jar and removed the silver cover. "Um, cottage cheese? I like cottage cheese."

She eyed the hungry cat. "I'll call you Stripe. Stripe, you must be very hungry, you're so greedy." She dumped all the cottage cheese on a smooth place beside the road and stood up. "Good-bye, Kitty. Doris is coming."

That evening Mama again praised Bea for eating all her lunch.

Bea opened her mouth to tell what really happened to her lunch. But just then Daddy yelled, "There goes Bell's heifer. It must have gotten out." Mama and Daddy both ran outside and chased the cow inside the fence by the barn, where Mr. Bell could come and get her.

Bea watched through the window, thinking, "Maybe Stripe won't be there again tomorrow morning. If Stripe doesn't come, I'll eat all my lunch if it chokes me and makes me sick."

Stripe came again. She came every morning. On Monday she growled. Bea felt sure she said in cat language how hungry a cat gets without food for two whole days.

Many days went by, and many times Bea should have told Mama and Daddy what really happened to part of her lunch, but she didn't. She felt guilty about it.

Stripe looked good now. Bea had all the burs picked out of her fur, and eating breakfast every morning made her feel better. She didn't yowl and mew anymore. She limped to Bea each morning and turned her purring machine on.

Bea loved Stripe and felt sorry she didn't have a home of her own.

Thanksgiving vacation came. Uncle Bill, Aunt Lucy, and the boys came for Thanksgiving dinner. Bea tried to stay away from Uncle Bill. She knew if he said that silly thing she wouldn't be able to answer, and he always said it. When they sat down for dinner, he looked across the table at Bea. "How's school? You have to talk there, don't you, Bea?"

Bea looked down at her plate.

Uncle Bill grinned. "I never thought the cat'd keep your tongue after you started to school."

Bea thought, "I'd like Uncle Bill if he wouldn't always say that." She was glad when dinner was over and they could go outside and play.

Bea didn't think about Stripe all day. She didn't think about her all vacation until Sunday morning. Then she worried, "Stripe must be half starved." She petted Puff Ball and whispered, "You know, Puffy, you're a very lucky cat. You have a home, a long tail, and all four legs."

Finally Bea went to her room and knelt by her bed. "Jesus, I didn't mean to tell a lie, but it is a lie, because I didn't tell where the food really went. It got harder and harder to tell. Now I can't tell without help. Please help me. I must tell Mama and Daddy, for Stripe is hungry. In Jesus name, Amen."

She stood up and went outside where Mama and Daddy were repairing a fence. She watched Mama hold the wire while Daddy pounded the nails. She sighed deeply and spoke up, "I must tell you something. It's important, so please don't run off before I get through."

Daddy stopped pounding. "Why, Sprout, do we really do that? I'm sure we never intended to. Fire away."

Bea straightened her shoulders and looked first at Daddy then at Mama. She said, "I want you to know, I never eat all my lunch."

Daddy put his hammer on the fence post and looked surprised. Mama said, "Go on, dear. Tell your story."

"Well, when I get out of the car and wait for Grandpa, a cat meets me. She has only three feet and half a tail. She's always hungry, and I feed her part of my lunch. She doesn't have a home."

Bea started to cry and ran into Mama's arms. "I didn't mean to let you think I ate all my lunch. It just got so I felt locked up every chance I had to tell you, just like when people say that about the cat's got my tongue. Now, Stripe's probably about starved, for I haven't fed her since Wednesday."

Mama hugged Bea close. "I guess we made it hard for you to tell us."

Daddy patted Bea on the shoulder. "If you can handle two cats and keep Stripe and Puff Ball from fighting, we'll go after Stripe. This farm's big enough for two cats. Just be sure and pinch us next time we don't listen. I'll put my tools away."

"Daddy! You're nice!" Bea squealed and ran to Daddy, giving him a big hug.

Bea and Daddy got into the car and drove to the crossroads. Bea jumped out of the car and started to call Stripe, but the cat came out of the bushes in big limps before she could say anything.

They took Stripe home and gave her food. Puff Ball didn't try to fight her. He didn't even raise the fur on his back. Stripe gulped milk and ate without paying much attention to Puff Ball.

Daddy said, "They're going to get along fine."

Bea took hold of Mama's and Daddy's hands. "I'll really try to eat all my lunch after this."

"All right, dear. That will be nice," Mama said.

Bea frowned. She had said she would talk to her teacher at the beginning of school, but it was weeks before she could. She must start right away eating all of her lunch.

Bea turned her attention to the animals. Mitzie ignored Stripe, But Storm yipped at her heels in an effort to get her to play.

Bea picked Storm up and called Mitzie. "Now, you dogs must be friends with Stripe. Understand?" She shook Storm a little. "Storm, you're getting to be a stinker. I don't want any mischief from you. Tomorrow, when I come home from school, I want a good report about you."

13. Runaway Puppy

Every afternoon Bea checked to see if her pets were getting along together. All four ran to greet her after school. They followed her everywhere. She said to Mama "We're five good friends. I like talking to them. I don't get frightened."

Days went fast. Bea thought Grandpa was right when he said everything happened in a hop, skip, and a jump from one thing to another. It had been a hop from Thanksgiving vacation to Christmas vacation, a skip and vacation was over, and now a jump put them into the deep January snow.

The snowplow came no farther than the crossroads, so the people around the lake and out in the country used sleds drawn by horses, for they couldn't drive their cars through the snow.

After vacation, when school started, Bea walked to the crossroads with Daddy; then Grandpa took her and Doris to school in a cutter drawn by his black mare, Lady. Bea liked riding in the cutter, for its thin metal runners skimmed swiftly over the snow-packed road.

After school Grandpa went around the lake by Bea's house to take her home. Sometimes he and Doris came inside to get warm and have a hot drink.

One afternoon when they stopped, Mama had cookies and hot chocolate for them. The girls played with the cats and raced around with Mitzie and Storm. When they left,

72 THE CAT'S GOT HER TONGUE

Doris waved and called, "Good-bye. See you in the morning."

Bea waved back and started helping Mama with dinner.

After dinner she fed the cats, then called Mitzie and Storm to their supper. Mitzie came right away as usual, but Storm didn't come.

"The little stinker's probably taking a nap somewhere," Daddy remarked.

Bea look under the couch and everywhere she could think of. No Storm!

"Try the bedrooms," Mama said.

With Daddy's help, Bea searched every room in the house.

"I must do the chores," Daddy said, buttoning up his coat. "Bea, get your coat and boots on. That pup must have sneaked outside. Maybe you can find him."

Daddy went out to the barn, and Bea looked all over the yard calling, "Storm, Storm. Come, Storm."

Mama opened the front door. "I'm letting Mitzie out. Maybe she'll find him."

Mitzie stood on the porch with one ear cocked, listening. She sniffed around the porch, down the steps, and out to where Lady had waited for Grandpa and Doris. She lifted her head, looked at Bea, and ran back into the house. Mama said, "Why can't you go farther than the driveway, Mitzie?"

Daddy and Bea came in without Storm. They searched inside again. Mama said, "He's not in the house."

Bea wailed. "Oh, my little Storm. He's caught in a trap. He'll freeze to death. His hair's so short it won't keep him warm."

Daddy frowned. "Now, Bea, don't make it any worse. He's a puppy. He won't go far. There aren't any traps on our farm. I'm going out to the barn to look again."

Daddy looked at Mama. She said, "Where could he be?"

"That's a stumper," Daddy replied and went outside. After a long time he came back without Storm. He reassured Bea, "Storm will whine at the door in a short time."

Bea spent the entire evening looking around, running to the window, and opening the door to call Storm.

Daddy didn't say once, "You're letting the cold air in."

Bedtime came. Mitzie jumped on the bed and cuddled close to Bea. Mama kissed Bea good-night and petted the dog. She didn't tell Mitzie to sleep where she belonged.

Bea prayed to Jesus, "We can't find Storm. You know where he is. Jesus, please take care of him. Bring little Storm home. Keep him safe. Amen."

In the morning, Bea asked if Storm came home. Mama looked sad and answered, "No."

Bea's lips began to quiver, "I know it doesn't change things to cry, but I love my little puppy."

"Breakfast is ready," Mama said.

Bea sat down with Daddy, but she couldn't eat. Daddy seemed to understand, for he didn't urge her to eat. He said, "Time to go. Bundle up well."

Bea blurted, "I'm not going to school."

"Yes, you are," Mama said firmly. "Hurry! There's Grandpa and Doris! I wonder why they came this way. How nice. You won't have to walk."

Doris jumped out of the cutter, and Grandpa followed her.

Mama opened the door.

Doris squealed. "Look, we had company last night." She held Storm out to Bea.

Everybody laughed as they scolded, petted, and cuddled Storm. When it quieted down, Grandpa said, "I did some grocery shopping before I picked up the girls yesterday afternoon. Sometime during our stop here, the little fellow must have gone outside. He smelled fresh meat in the cutter and followed his nose. When we got home I found him fast asleep. The bag was open, and the paper was torn off the meat. He had eaten until his tummy pouched out, then gone to sleep. There are no phones out our way, so we couldn't call you. Doris had a puppy for the night."

Daddy said, "I'm glad you had him. There have been some unhappy people here."

Mama explained. "Mitzie followed his trail out to where Lady stood, but that's as far as she could find his scent."

Bea held Storm close. "Good-bye, you naughty puppy. I must go to school."

Bea was careful not to let Storm out the door when they left.

Bea and Daddy climbed into the back of the cutter. She liked having Daddy ride with them. She bubbled inside with happiness because Storm was home. She thanked Jesus over and over in her mind.

Time passed quickly at school. After lunch, the teacher took all the children out in the yard to make snowmen. When they came in, Miss Harvey read a book about Abraham Lincoln, because it would soon be his birthday, and he had been a good man.

After school, while Doris and Bea waited out front for Grandpa, Jimmy and some other boys walked by. Jimmy came close to Bea and threw snow in her face. She spluttered and wiped her face. Jimmy laughed. "What's the matter, twerp? Are you afraid to say anything?"

She was glad when Grandpa came.

The girls rode in the cutter for just a few more weeks after that, for the snow and ice started to melt. Streams of water flowed along the road, and some ran across it from the melting snow. Everybody called it the thaw. The thaw lasted several weeks; then the water dried up in the road and Daddy could use the car.

The girls again met at the crossing and walked to school. Time went by. They enjoyed the early spring weather. Everything seemed the same, but one Thursday was different.

14. A Lost Envelope

On the Thursday morning that was different, Bea explained to Daddy, "It's funny. Teachers go to school today, but we don't. Guess what! Doris and I are going on a picnic all by ourselves."

Daddy raised his eyebrows. "What's this you're planning?"

"We're going to take important papers to Mr. Kramer for Doris's grandpa. If you go in a car, you must go clear to town and out another road to reach Kramer's. Our Lake Road doesn't go there. We're going on an old trail road on Grandpa's land. It's much shorter. We can walk."

Daddy said, "Be careful. That's a long way for two little girls, even if you are nearly second graders."

"We'll be careful," Bea promised.

"OK. I'll take you to Grandpa's on my way to work." Mama handed Bea her lunch. "I put two of everything in. Be in Grandpa's yard when Daddy comes by for you. He will come that way after work."

Bea jumped from the car at Doris's house. The girls grabbed hands and whirled around.

Doris's mother came out and handed Doris her lunch. "I put two of everything in," she said.

Bea laughed. "That's what my Mama did. We'll have two picnics."

Grandpa gave Doris a brown envelope. "Calm down.

This paper is important. Don't use it for a boat in the creek."

"Gran-n-n-d pa-a-a, I wouldn't," Doris wailed.

Grandpa roughed the back of both girls' hair, "Probably not, but when you two get together you're a little scatterbrained. Now, with all your fiddlin' and exploring you ought to be home around three o'clock. I'm glad you tell time. Look at your watch once in a while, Doris. That'll keep you in line."

The girls said good-bye, went around the house and over the back fence, then followed a trail through pine trees until they came to an old logging road. Grass grew high in the middle and sides, making it look like two trails. They hurried along for some time. Suddenly they exclaimed together, "Oh," as a little brown bunny dashed in front of them. They looked through the grass and all over, but they couldn't see where he went.

Bea said, "He was here and then gone."

They continued on their way. Later Doris pointed. "Look at the old house. It's almost gone. No one's lived there for a long time. Grandpa said they moved to town many years ago."

They pushed through tall ferns toward the wide, gaping entrance where the door had fallen off. They walked over the door and headed for some rickety old stairs. "Maybe there's a treasure up here," Bea said in a whisper. But all they found was a small platform at the top of the stairs and a pile of hazelnut shells.

"I guess the squirrels had their dinner here," Doris said.

Some narrow boards had been nailed from the platform across the room below. The ceiling was gone.

"I wonder how far I can go out on these boards," Bea said. "I'll pretend I'm a tight-rope walker."

She walked a few steps and looked down. What a long way! Her legs began to shake, and she felt she might fall. She sat down and scooted out to the middle.

Doris yelled, "Some tight-rope walker you are!"

The board began to creak and sway. It might break! She could feel it bend! "Doris! It's going to break!"

"Come back! Quick! Maybe you can make it."

Bea held her breath. She could feel the board giving under her. She moved toward Doris as fast as she could. The board still creaked and swayed. It was hard to go backward, but she was afraid to turn around. As she neared the platform the board swayed less.

Doris grabbed under her arms and pulled her off the board. Bea gasped, "What if the board had broken! I promised Daddy to be careful."

"Well, it didn't break," Doris said. "I'm glad of that. Let's go."

They went down the stairs to a little creek with grass along the edge and sat down. Bea said, "Let's eat one of the lunches."

"All right," Doris agreed. "I'll put one in each hand behind me, and you choose the one we'll eat."

Bea chose the left one, which was hers. Each girl had a luscious sandwich, a cupcake, and an orange.

After eating, Bea picked up Doris's lunch. "We'll take turns carrying it."

They came to a wire fence and crawled under. Later they had to climb over a board fence.

"There's Kramers'." Doris pointed.

"Another field and we'll be there," Bea sighed.

The girls had been trading about, carrying Doris's lunch. Doris handed it to Bea, "Your turn."

She looked at her empty hands and then at Bea's hands holding the lunch bag. "Bea! The important papers! They're gone!"

Bea stared at Doris, startled. "Didn't you take care of them? How dumb!"

Doris's face flushed. "Oh! I'm dumb. I don't go on rickety old boards playing tight-roper! You certainly could have helped me." Tears ran down Doris's face. "What will Grandpa say?"

Bea felt like crying too, but she said, "Don't cry, Doris.

I'm sorry. We'll find it. Maybe it's on the road or where we climbed the fence."

Doris added, "Or where we ate."

"Or by the old house," Bea said.

The girls groaned together. "Such a long way!"

"Come on," Bea said. "You look on that side and I'll look on this side."

Tired and hot, they searched where they ate their lunch and scanned the bushes near the old house. They went inside and hunted on the stairs and platform. They couldn't find the important papers.

Bea said, "We had the envelope when we stopped here. We put the lunches down, and you leaned it against the wall."

"That's right."

Bea stopped. "Jesus knows where those important papers are. Let's ask Him to help us."

Doris said, "You pray if you think it will help."

They knelt in the tall grass, and Bea prayed, "Jesus, we've been careless with Grandpa's important papers. We should have been more careful with them. We're sorry. Please help us find them. Thank You. Amen."

They stood and started toward Kramers' again. They came to the creek and Bea suggested, "Let's wash our faces. I'm hot." They splashed in the cold water and used their skirts for towels.

Doris said, "I'm hungry again. If we eat my lunch, we won't have to carry it.

Bea agreed and picked up the lunch. They sat in the cool grass by the creek and Bea opened the sack, reached in, and then looked at Doris as if shocked.

Doris said, "What's the matter?"

Bea pulled the brown envelope with the important papers in it from the bag.

Doris wailed, "Oh, I remember now! I put it in there one time when it was my turn to carry the lunch." She grabbed the sack and envelope. They started walking again, neither one thinking about eating.

A LOST ENVELOPE 79

Bea's face flushed. She felt unhappy with Doris. It was a long way back to where they turned around. She wanted to frown and close her mouth tight. She forgot about Jesus, and never once offered to carry the sack.

They walked fast and sometimes ran. They climbed over the fences and went through fields and at last knocked at the door of a brown house with flowers in the front yard.

A man answered the door and invited them in. Doris gave him the envelope and said she was to wait for an answer.

Mrs. Kramer gave each girl a glass of lemonade. She asked them, "What grade are you in?"

Doris answered, "We're both in the first grade."

The lady asked, "Are you neighbors?"

Doris said, "We live across the lake from each other."

The lady and Doris kept talking. Mrs. Kramer often looked at Bea as if she expected her to enter the conversation. Bea thought she seemed to be a nice lady, but that tight feeling crept up her throat and she couldn't say anything.

Mr. Kramer wrote his name on the paper, wrote a note, and put everything back in the envelope and gave it to Doris. He said, "Thank you for bringing this to me. Be careful with it."

Doris glanced at Bea but never mentioned that they had lost the papers in the lunch sack.

Mrs. Kramer said to her husband, "They're nice girls, but this one doesn't talk."

Mr. Kramer laughed and looked at Bea. "I bet the cat's got her tongue."

Bea walked to the door and outside with her lips tight.

Doris said, "Good-bye," and they started home.

After they climbed the second fence, Doris said, "Bea, why won't you talk sometimes?"

Bea couldn't answer right away. Would Doris bother her about that all the time? Finally she said, "I can't, especially when they say that about the cat."

Doris replied, "They wouldn't say it if you talked."

Bea closed her mouth and walked in silence.

Doris looked at her watch, "It's two thirty. We'd better hurry." They walked without stopping until they arrived at Doris's house. Doris gave Grandpa the envelope. He thanked them and hurried off somewhere in his old Ford.

They sat under a tree to rest and finish their picnic.

"Just think, school will soon be out," Doris said.

"Yes, and we'll be second graders," Bea replied.

Doris said, "And you know, Bea, you must answer people when they speak to you, now that we'll be in the second grade."

Just then Daddy came by and honked. Bea said goodbye and ran out to the car. On the way home she thought to herself, "Is Doris going into that thing about talking? If she ever says that about the cat, I'll never be friends with her again."

15. The Bible Meetings

After that Thursday, Doris never mentioned Bea's problem about talking to people. This made Bea happy, for she loved her friend.

Everything seemed wonderful. Vacation came. The miracle happened. Caterpillars were butterflies and Bea was beginning to read *Our Little Friend.* One thing still worried her. Mama didn't have Sabbath School. Daddy seemed happy she could read, but he never talked about the lessons in the paper she read. Maybe it took a long time. "I won't give up," she promised herself.

One day Mama said a second grader could walk around the lake to Doris's house and play. On the way Bea went by the little, empty one-room schoolhouse. Children had gone to school there a long time ago. Someone had cut the grass around the building. The windows gleamed clean in the sun. Bea could see a man and woman walking around inside. She wondered to herself, "What's going on? Why have they cleaned everything? Is someone going to live in the old schoolhouse?"

Bea told Doris about the schoolhouse. "It looks as if something's going to happen there. What do you suppose it is?"

"I wonder," Doris said.

When it was time for Bea to go home, Doris's mother said that to satisfy her curiosity, Doris could walk with Bea to the schoolhouse.

The girls stopped in front of the building. Bea noticed that while they played at Doris's house, someone had put a huge sign on the side of the school. It said, "Bible Prophecy Explained."

A friendly lady came down the steps and smiled at them. "I'm Mrs. Morris. Tell me your names."

Without thinking about being shy, Bea told her name right along with Doris and asked, "What does the sign mean?"

Mrs. Morris explained, "Every night we will have meetings and talk about Jesus. There will be Bible stories for the children. Be sure and tell your friends to come. The meetings start Friday night at seven o'clock."

Doris told Mrs. Morris they would try to come. Then Mrs. Morris went inside. Before the girls said good-bye to each other, Doris laughed. "You talked to that grown-up lady."

Bea laughed too. "It was easy. She's a Jesus lady."

Bea raced home to tell Mama about the meetings. "May we go?" she asked.

"Well," Mama hesitated. "Of course, we know nothing about this church. I wouldn't care to go to just any church."

"She's a nice lady, Mama."

Mama explained, "Many nice people belong to churches other than the Seventh-day Adventist Church. However, they may teach rules men have made instead of God's rules."

Later in the evening Mama said to Daddy, "Please drive down past the little school. Bea is excited about a mystery there. See if you can find out what's going on. Take her with you, of course."

Daddy laughed. "OK. Come on, Curiosity."

Bea climbed into the car with Daddy. He drove to the little school and stopped. He studied the sign and said in a kind but firm voice, "That's a Seventh-day Adventist sign. They will have meetings about the Bible. You and your mother may go if you like. I'll stay away. I must

THE BIBLE MEETINGS 83

work on Saturday. If I go to the meetings, I will believe what they say. In fact, I do believe what they say. But I can't be a Sabbath keeper and work where I do. I need my job to take care of you and Mama."

Bea glanced at Daddy. He looked sad and seemed to be talking to himself.

She said no more about the meetings, but she thought about them. She wanted to go, and she wanted Mama and Daddy to go.

Friday, Bea couldn't help saying, "Mama, let's go to the meeting. There's a Bible story for children."

"Oh, we might as well go," Mama said. "However, Daddy won't go."

That evening Bea looked around the schoolroom. Old-fashioned desks stayed in place, row by row. She could see books on the top of the cupboard. One book had a picture of Jesus on the cover. A magazine had a picture of many stars in the sky. She remembered reading in *Our Little Friend* about the stars in the sky falling like that. It had happened. It meant Jesus would come soon.

The teacher's desk stood in the front at one side. An old battered piano faced it from the other side. Between the desk and the piano was a tall stand.

The minister placed his Bible on the stand. He smiled and greeted everyone. Then he said, "Shall we stand for prayer." After prayer he played the piano and Mrs. Morris sang with the people from a book called *Gospel Songs*.

The Bible story came next. Mrs. Morris told about Adam and Eve. Bea felt sorry Adam and Eve disobeyed God. She thought, "Just think, if they hadn't eaten the fruit God told them to stay away from, everyone would be good. Everybody would be happy. Little Dale would be alive."

Bea smiled. Even if people sinned, Jesus forgave them. He'd come again and take all His people to heaven.

It seemed as if Mr. Morris talked a long time, but Bea kept very quiet. She wanted Mama to hear every word.

Bea counted the people. There were twelve grown-ups

and five children at the meeting. She wished more would come. She'd try to get Doris to come the next night. She wished Mildred and her parents hadn't moved away. They might have come and brought all the little ones.

After the closing song and prayer, Mr. and Mrs. Morris stood at the door and shook hands with everyone. Mrs. Morris squeezed Bea's hand and said, "I knew you would come." Bea got a nice warm feeling all over. She liked Mrs. Morris.

Mama and Bea walked home from the meeting. Mama didn't talk, but the stars twinkled down at Bea. They seemed to flash a message from Jesus, "Everything's going to be all right. Just wait."

16. Visiting an Enemy

The day after the meeting, Bea asked, "Mama, shall we go tonight? I liked the story. Mrs. Morris said if I come every night I'll hear the whole Bible story."

"Why do you insist, Bea? It will only cause quarreling in the family."

"Daddy said he doesn't care if we go."

"Of course he wouldn't care if we go, but when the Daddy in the family doesn't keep the Sabbath and the Mama does, it causes irritation."

"But Daddy will someday," Bea promised. "I pray to Jesus about it."

Mama sighed, "Oh, all right."

Bea wanted Doris to hear the Bible stories too. She ran most of the way around the lake to invite her to go with them.

Doris said, "Mother already belongs to a church. Her beliefs are different, and she'll probably say No."

Doris's mother shook her head, but Grandpa said, "Doris should learn what other people believe. I'll come by the schoolhouse when the meeting's over and walk home with her."

It was agreed. Doris had permission to go. The girls walked along the road under the big pine trees to Bea's house. On the way, Bea told Doris the story she had heard the night before.

That evening as they entered the building Mrs. Morris

beamed on the girls and said to Bea, "How nice you brought your friend tonight."

The two girls listened to the story about baby Moses. Bea thought, "It's important to follow God's rules. God takes care of His people."

After the meeting Grandpa met Doris at the door. Mr. Morris talked to him in a friendly way. Bea felt happy. Maybe Grandpa would come and bring Doris every night.

They went to three more meetings, but Doris didn't come.

One morning Bea, with Mitzie and Storm, went out under the three cedars. Bea sat in her swing and prayed, "Jesus, Doris doesn't know the Bible stories very well. Please have her come tonight. Amen." She opened her eyes and said to Mitzie and Storm, "Doris will come. Jesus will arrange it."

As if happy with this information, the dogs ran around Bea barking joyously until she ran with them to the edge of the pasture and back.

That evening, Bea looked around the schoolroom for Doris, and there she sat with Grandpa. The girls ran to greet each other. They grabbed hands and swung back and forth giggling. Bea said, "I prayed for you to come."

Doris answered, "I did too. When I asked Mother, she said No, but Grandpa said he'd like to come. So here we are."

The girls sat in one of the big desks together. They listened quietly. The story was about God writing His rules on a table of stone. Mrs. Morris said, "God's rules will make you happy if you obey them."

Bea sat still during the sermon. It seemed very long. She felt like wiggling and whispering to Doris. She didn't, though. Mama might never come again if she acted naughty.

Suddenly Bea heard something that made her sit up very straight. Mr. Morris said, "If you are kind to your enemies, they often become your best friends. Jesus was never unkind. He prayed for His enemies. His kindness

VISITING AN ENEMY 87

made people want to follow Him. That's why the thief on the cross believed in Jesus."

After the meeting, Bea whispered to Doris and Doris whispered back. Bea squeezed Doris's hand. "Let's do it."

Doris agreed. "Let's. Grandpa will help us think of something."

Bea whispered again, "We must pray too. Jesus will make it happen."

The following day, the girls had a prayer meeting in Doris's pasture. Doris prayed, "You know, God, that Bea and I didn't light the fire at the party last year. Jimmy told a lie about us. He is our enemy, but we want to be kind to him. Amen."

Bea prayed, "Dear Jesus, we want to be kind to our enemy. Jimmy is our enemy. He made the grown-ups at the party think we were bad. He called us twerps and said we had matches. Doris and I want to be kind to him. Please help us. Amen."

They stood and brushed the grass off their bare knees. Then they ran to the house hunting Grandpa. They found him reading the paper. He listened to their story and said, "I knew Jimmy's dad when he was a boy. He acted the same way, always doing tricks and blaming others."

Doris said, "We want to be nice to Jimmy, even if he is bad."

"So, you want to be kind to Jimmy? What do you want to do for him?"

"We don't know," Doris answered.

Grandpa inquired, "Well, what would make Jimmy a better boy?"

Bea spoke up, "If he knew Jesus."

Doris looked at Bea and Bea looked at Doris. Bea burst out in one breath, "I know. We can ask him to the meetings. He can listen to the Bible stories."

Doris exclaimed, "That's it! But where does he live? Do you know, Grandpa?"

"Yes, I know. Of course, his dad might not take him, and he might not go anyway, but I'll take you in my old

Ford. You can ask him. Hurry! I want to get back in time for the meeting. I liked the one last night."

Doris ran and told her mother where they were going.

Grandpa took them clear past their school and down a side road. He stopped the car in front of a nice farmhouse. He said, "Here we are. This is the place, girls. Hop out. I hope it works."

Bea said, "Oh, Doris! I'm afraid! Maybe I won't be able to say anything. You'll have to do the talking."

Doris replied, "I'm afraid too. You go with us, Grandpa. You ask him."

"Oh, no! This is not my idea. Where's all this excitement about helping your enemy? You'd better hurry. I'm not coming again, and we don't have much time. Just tell him there are meetings down at the old Lake Schoolhouse, the stories are good, and you thought he would like to come."

Bea took hold of Doris's hand, and they climbed out of the car. They had a hard time getting the gate open, and a huge gray dog ran out barking at them.

Jimmy's father came out to the porch and yelled, "Buster! Shut up! Get over here and be quiet!"

He laughed and looked down at the girls. "He won't hurt you. What do you little sweethearts want?"

Bea didn't like being called sweetheart, and the dog frightened her. She squeezed her hot hands into fists and cleared her throat. She felt all locked up.

The man said, "Did you want something?"

Bea looked at Doris. Doris wasn't going to say a thing. She was watching the dog. She looked as if she might run back to Grandpa. Bea thought, "Oh, my, how can I ever be a missionary? How can I help an enemy? Jesus, help me. Please, help me." Then plain as anybody she said, "We want to see Jimmy."

"You do? Come on in," the man blustered.

Bea and Doris followed him inside. He raised his voice louder than ever, "Jimmy, come on downstairs. Some friends are here to see you."

Jimmy took his time coming. He stood in front of the girls and grumbled, "What do you want?"

Doris whispered to Bea, "You tell him, Bea."

What was the matter with Doris? She always did the talking for them. She knew about Bea's problem with talking to people. Bea shut her eyes for a second right in front of them all. "Help me again, Jesus," she prayed in her mind.

Bea took a deep breath and looked up at Jimmy's father, who still stood near by. Then she looked at Jimmy and took another deep breath. Her voice quivered, but she said, "Jimmy, we want to be kind to you."

Oh, she shouldn't have said that.

Jimmy looked surprised.

Bea took another deep breath. "We came to tell you about the meetings in the old Lake Schoolhouse. They have them every night at seven o'clock."

"And stories for the children," Doris ventured to say.

Jimmy looked at them both without answering.

Jimmy's father laughed. "Well, that's nice of you little sweethearts to ask Jimmy."

The girls turned and ran out the door to the car. The big gray dog ran behind them all the way. Grandpa helped them into the car, and they went on their way.

"The most terrible thing!" Doris spluttered. "Jimmy never said a word, except, 'What do you want?'"

"His father called us sweethearts," Bea said.

Grandpa laughed. "What do you care? You got the message to him, I hope?"

Doris sniffed with tears in her eyes. "Yes, but he didn't say a thing, only stared."

Bea put her arm around Doris. "Don't cry. We did missionary work. We did the kindest thing we could think of to our enemy. And, Doris, Jesus helped me talk. It was hard, but with Jesus' help, I did. I wonder if Jimmy will come."

17. "Let's Go, Daddy!"

It took time for the girls to calm down after they asked Jimmy to the meetings, but they decided to let Jesus take care of things.

Bea had dinner with Doris; then they went to the meeting with Grandpa. What a surprise! Bea's grandma was sitting by Mama.

Grandma cuddled Bea close and said, "This must be Doris," and put her arm around Doris too.

Grandma went to the meetings with Bea and Mama after that. Every evening, Bea looked around for Jimmy, but he didn't come.

One evening before the meeting, Bea read lessons from her stack of *Our Little Friends* to Grandma. Daddy came in and sat down with them. After one of the lessons, Grandma said, "A nice little missionary like Bea ought to have her daddy in church with her."

Daddy smiled, "Oh, you're in it too, are you?"

Grandma replied, "Yes, and you'd better get in too. It's the truth, you know."

Bea climbed on Daddy's lap. "Come, Daddy, come with us. It will be lots of fun in heaven if we're all there together. Please come to the meeting tonight."

Daddy looked at Grandma. "She's been reading that *Our Little Friend* of hers to me ever since she started learning words. Guess I'll go tonight, at least. I have to please my young sprout once in a while."

Daddy, Mama, and Grandma went with Bea to three more meetings. Then they went to the fourth one. Doris sat by Bea. She reached out and pushed Bea's arm. "Look! Look!"

Bea glanced back. Jimmy, his little brother, his mother, and his father walked in the doorway. The girls looked away quickly to be polite.

Bea could feel goose bumps forming on her arms. She thought, "Mama, Daddy, and my grandma, Doris and her grandpa, and now Jimmy and his family. Jesus listened to my prayers. He always does."

She smiled to herself. "Jesus, Jesus, Thank You for everything."

The meeting came to an end. Everyone talked a long time. Daddy and Jimmy's father shook hands. Mama talked to Jimmy's mother.

Jimmy said to the girls, "Hi, twerps."

Bea didn't get angry about being called a twerp. What difference did it make? Jimmy had come to the meeting, and he had spoken to them. She laughed and said, "Hi, I'm glad you came."

Bea could hardly believe all the good things that happened after that. Jimmy and his family came every night to all the meetings. Daddy came every night too.

It seemed as if the more she learned about Jesus the more she wanted to tell others about Him. The more she talked about Jesus, the easier it was to speak to everyone. No one said anymore, "The cat's got her tongue." She reasoned to herself, "If Uncle Bill says it again, I'll just laugh and say, 'The cat gave it back to me.'"

The days were happy too. Bea watched Grandma when she stood up from sitting in the rocking chair. She wasn't a bit careful. She let the chair rock with no one in it. She didn't look frightened. How strange!

Bea thought it might be an accident. Maybe Grandma forgot. She put a needle on the floor pointing toward the kitchen where Grandma would see it when she came into the other room. She knew at one time Grandma would go around the needle and pick it up from the other end and say, "I don't want this needle pointing at me. I have enough trouble." But this time Grandma didn't say a thing. She picked the needle up and put it in Mama's sewing box.

Another nice thing happened. When Bea talked about little Dale, Grandma never mentioned the little lost bird or pursed her lips together.

One evening Grandma suggested they walk to the meeting. Bea liked walking with Grandma. She never once said to be careful of a black cat or any other silly thing. She didn't seem to be afraid of anything. Grandma was not superstitious anymore.

After the sermon, the preacher asked the people to come up to the front of the room if they wanted to follow Jesus. Mama and Grandma went. Bea prayed, "Thank You, Jesus. Now I know we'll have Sabbath School again."

Doris and Grandpa followed Mama and Grandma. "How wonderful," Bea thought. "Now we can all have Sabbath School together."

Bea looked up at Daddy. She wanted Daddy to follow Jesus. "Let's go, Daddy!" she said.

Daddy squeezed Bea's hand, and they went together. Bea felt she would explode with happiness. Daddy would keep Sabbath too. He could find another job.

As they walked home, Bea looked up at the sky. "Someday Mama, Grandma, Daddy, little Dale, and I will go together past the bright twinkly stars. We will be on our way to heaven with Jesus. I love You, Jesus. Thank You."